BOY O'BOY

BRIAN DOYLE

Boy O'Boy

A GROUNDWOOD BOOK
DOUGLAS & McINTYRE
TORONTO VANCOUVER BERKELEY

Groundwood Books / Douglas & McIntyre
720 Bathurst Street, Suite 500, Toronto, Ontario M5S 2R4

Distributed in the USA by Publishers Group West
1700 Fourth Street, Berkeley, CA 94710

We acknowledge for their financial support of our publishing program the Canada Council for the Arts, the Government of Canada through the Book Publishing Industry Development Program (BPIDP), the Ontario Arts Council and the Government of Ontario through the Ontario Media Development Corporation's Ontario Book Initiative.

ONTARIO ARTS COUNCIL
CONSEIL DES ARTS DE L'ONTARIO

National Library of Canada Cataloging in Publication
Doyle, Brian
Boy O'Boy / by Brian Doyle.
ISBN 0-88899-588-1 (bound).–ISBN 0-88899-590-3 (pbk.)
I. Title.
PS8557.O87B69 2003   jC813'.54   C2003-902985-9
PZ7

Cover photography by Tim Fuller
Design by Michael Solomon

Printed and bound in Canada

Acknowledgments

The writer of a tale always needs other people's help to get it right. I would like to thank Marilyn Kennedy for processing the material and keeping it on track; Mike Paradis for his sharp-eyed editing and helpful feedback; Desmond Hassell of Parkdale United Church, Ottawa, for his pipe organ instruction; and my longtime partner in concocting musicals and other illegal products, Stanley Clark, who trained my ears to hear "Crown Imperial."

I am also indebted to Jeanne Safer's excellent study, *The Normal One: Life With a Difficult or Damaged Sibling* (The Free Press, New York, 2002).

This book is dedicated to my sister Fay, of Peggy's Cove, Nova Scotia, and my brother Mike, of Clayton, Ontario. And to Sandy Farquharson, who wears a sleep mask. And to Debra Joynt, of Chelsea School, a great teacher.

Contents

1

Baron Strathcona's Fountain

MY GRANNY died last night. "Death will come and take her tonight." That's what they said. Death came and Granny died. But she was still there. Death didn't take her away. It was a big black car that came and took her away.

I was named after her. Her name was Martina. I am Martin. No *a* on the end. My last name is O'Boy. I'm Martin O'Boy. Some people try to call me Boy O'Boy. But I don't like it.

My father was sleeping downstairs on the couch with the spring sticking up. My mother was sleeping on the floor beside the bed upstairs where Granny was. This morning early before the sun came up the men came and got Granny and drove her away in a big black car.

Now, I guess, my mother and father can go back to their own bed.

Last night we were all standing beside the bed: Dr.

O'Malley, Father Fortier, my mother, my father, my twin brother, Phil, and Cheap, my cat.

My granny stopped breathing. I heard the last breath she let out. It was a long breath. Like a long sigh.

Oh...

Dear...

Me.

It sounded like she was very, very tired. So tired.

Father Fortier was saying the words.

Dr. O'Malley was nodding his nods.

A few hours later I went back in to see her. To see my granny.

The doctor and the priest were gone. Phil, my twin, was asleep. My mother and father were down in the kitchen, arguing, but not very loud.

I go in to see Granny.

The light from the hallway cuts into the room. Her dark shape. There on the bed. Is she breathing? No. The bed, did it creak? No. Darker than night on the other side of the room.

Her legs feel hard like logs floating in the river. Arms like the marble of a statue. Cement feet. Hands like stone. Fingers like carrots in the dark cold storage. Her face of glass — cold, thick glass.

My granny dead. Her hair like silk. Her head like the heads of the iron soldiers at the war monument...

The men came and covered her and put her on a stretcher and they grunted and groaned with her all the way down our narrow stairs when they carried her.

I remember Granny specially in the winter when she'd come over almost every day. She lived on Robinson Avenue over in Overbrook near the slaughterhouse. She used to walk all the way down to our house almost every day from there. Past the slaughterhouse, down the path through the thick, tall dark tunnel of bush along the Rideau River, through Strathcona Park, up to Baron Strathcona's fountain, over to Rideau Street and down Cobourg Street, past Heney Park to the corner of Papineau Street and our place.

Granny was very beautiful, even though she was old. She had long, long curly hair and big blue eyes. My twin brother Phil would run to the door when she came in and so did I.

We'd feel her cold fur coat with some of the fur out of it and I'd laugh at her fogged-up glasses. When she came into the hot hallway out of the cold her glasses would fog up right away and she wouldn't be able to see a thing.

"Ah canna see a thing," she'd say. "Ah canna see but ah ken it's ye wee 'uns!"

She talked that way because she was from Scotland.

And we'd feel her coat and I'd reach in her pockets and look for candy she always had there and I'd put her umbrella in the corner for her and help her take off her coat.

And my twin brother Phil would have a candy in his hand and start howling for somebody to take the paper off for him.

Granny always had her umbrella with her. Even in the winter. The black umbrella with the very sharp point on the end.

My mother once told me that a long time ago one summer around when I was born a man came out of the slaughterhouse and started following Granny down the path along the Rideau River and she started walking faster and so did he and she started running with her long hair flying and he was running too and she had her umbrella with her because it looked like rain and she stopped suddenly and turned around and stabbed him in the face with the black umbrella with the very sharp point on the end and he bent over with his hands covering his face and then she ran up to Baron Strathcona's fountain and stopped there to get her breath and she turned around and looked back and he was gone and maybe she poked out one of his eyes...

And so after that she always had her umbrella with her, rain or shine, summer or winter.

I often picked up the umbrella and played with it. Playing sword with it.

In the last few days of school this year before the summer holidays the teacher, Miss Gilhooly, was trying to waste time. She made us draw a picture of some summer *activity* that we would be *involved* in when the holidays came, if they ever did come, something that we could *imagine* we would be *involved* in.

So I drew a picture of a beautiful lady with long hair driving a sword right into the eye of a ghoul with blood and jelly squirting out and the ghoul shouting, screaming, "EEEEE!" in big red letters and a slaughterhouse behind and Baron Strathcona's fountain right there.

Everybody in the class got their picture back but me.

Then school was over.

And sometimes when Granny came visiting, she brought Grampa with her. He's from Scotland too. He never said anything so I never knew if he talked funny like Granny but he probably did.

In Scotland when he was young he was a famous soccer player. In the summer in our little yard, I'd throw my rubber ball at him and he'd bounce it back to me with his bald head. He could make the ball go anywhere you wanted it to go.

We hung a barrel hoop on our apple tree that never has any apples on it and he used to bounce the ball through the hoop with his head every time.

In the house in the winter he could hit our cat, Cheap, every time with the ball, but if Granny caught him doing that she'd yell at him.

"Dinna do thot!"

He never said anything back. He'd just smile.

And sometimes he'd look at me for a long, long time until I would get feeling strange and I'd leave the room.

I have so much curly blond hair and he has none — not one hair on his head. Was that what he was thinking? That he'd like to have some hair?

Then he got a stroke and now he's in the Home sitting in a chair looking out the window all day long. I wonder, when we sometimes go to visit him, what he's thinking now, looking out the window.

My father says he probably wishes he was back in Scotland.

In the Highlands.

That's where his heart is, my mother says. I like that. When she says that. About where your heart is.

I don't know where my heart is.

2

The Turkey Lady
and the Ketchup Lady

I'M SITTING on our front step hugging my knees. We have no veranda. Just a cement step and then the sidewalk. Our door is two doors down from Cobourg Street, on Papineau Street.

I'm thinking about a few things. I'm thinking about how the war is almost over and how every day now there's soldiers and sailors and air force men coming home and there's always parties in the streets at night.

And I'm thinking about my birthday coming soon and I'm wondering if I'll get a present this year. Last year I got a cat with one ear for my birthday.

And also I'm thinking about tonight when I get to go to sing in the Protestant church choir on King Edward up the hill past Rideau Street from the Little Theatre.

Two ladies come along.

I sit and look at them. It's morning right around the time when the ice truck comes. When the truck comes I can reach in the back — the driver lets me do it — and get a piece of ice to suck. It tastes like ice but it smells like wood and wet sawdust.

But I can't go to the truck now because of these ladies standing in front of me, talking to me. The truck is delivering next door to Mrs. Sawyer. We don't get the ice delivered because it's too expensive. It's cheaper if I go to the ice house with the wagon and get it myself.

A streetcar goes by on Cobourg. One of the tall ones. With the long face. He says Cobourg Barns on his forehead. His eyes are the tall windows. His little round nose is the headlight. His mouth is the catcher. He's not smiling. He never smiles.

"You must be Martin," one of the ladies says.

The ladies have beautiful clothes on. They both have colored umbrellas but it's not raining anymore. The sun is out and there's steam coming off the streetcar tracks and parts of the sidewalk.

Sometimes the water truck comes along and washes the street. I like to sit on the curb and let the water spraying from the truck splash on my feet. But this steam is because of the rain, not the water truck.

The street smells clean.

Our step is broken in half. I'm sitting on the higher part. I have on socks and over the socks I'm wearing rubbers. I have no shoes. My rubbers are held on by elastics the same color as the socks and the rubbers. Black. My legs are white. Except for the scabs on my knees from falling on the road playing soccer with a tennis ball with Billy Batson. The scabs are brown and red. My short pants are brown. I have a pocket in the left side but there's nothing in it. I have on a white undershirt. My sweater is wool and the color is gray. It's getting hot so I'll take it off but I can't right now because these two ladies are here now, looking down at me.

The cuffs of my sweater are coming apart. The threads of wool are hanging down. With my fingers I pull up the threads and close my hands around them so the ladies can't see. I look like I have no hands.

The ladies squeeze up their faces when the streetcar goes by. They can feel the rumbling of the streetcar up through their fancy shiny shoes and up their legs inside their dresses.

One of the ladies has some wrinkles around her mouth and loose skin on her neck like a turkey. And she has blue hair. A turkey with blue hair.

The other lady has hair the color of peaches piled up with curls and her cheeks are painted pink and her eyelashes are long and black and her eyes are like blueberries and her lips are painted with heavy thick lipstick the color of ketchup.

The turkey lady has a watch hanging on her chest beside her glasses hanging there too. I can tell the time on the watch even though it's upside down.

It's a quarter after eight.

"We're very sorry to hear about your grandmother. She went to sleep last night, didn't she?" the ketchup lady says in a sing-songy voice.

"She didn't go to sleep," I say. "She died."

"Ah, yes, that's it, Martin, isn't it?" says the turkey lady. I'm being impudent and I know it.

Our door opens and my cat, Cheap, gets pushed out to sit beside me.

"Oh, what an interesting cat!" says the ketchup lady. "What's it's name?"

"Cheap," I say. "I got him for my birthday last year. My father bought him at Radmore's pet shop on Rideau Street for ten cents because of his missing ear. Cheap."

"Oh," says the ketchup lady. She's smiling but she doesn't want to.

"Are those your shoes?" says the turkey lady.

"They're not shoes, they're rubbers," I say.

"Where did you get all that lovely curly hair?" says the ketchup lady.

"Where'd you get your hair?" I say. Impudent.

My granny would say, "Dinna be impudent."

"How old are you?" says the turkey lady.

They always ask you how old you are. But you're not allowed to ask them how old they are.

I don't tell her. She goes into her purse and takes out a paper and unfolds it.

"Did you draw this? Martin? In school? Mmm?"

A beautiful lady stabbing a ghoul is the picture.

"EEEEEE!"

3

Papineau Street and the Aztecs

THE FAMILY allowance check came today. I saw the mailman come and give it to my mother not too long after the turkey lady and the ketchup lady left the house.

My mother got Phil ready and walked up to the bank on Rideau Street to cash the check. Each month we get sixteen dollars. Eight dollars for each kid in the family.

Phil gets the same as me even though he's not the same as me.

I'm trying to figure out how much money Horseball Laflamme's mother gets from the mailman. They have so many kids she must get lots of money. They all live next door to us at number one Papineau. There's something wrong with Horseball's father, Mr. Laflamme. He coughs a lot at night. You can hear him through our bedroom wall upstairs. Coughing and hacking and spitting.

We live at number three Papineau.

Next door to us at number five is Buz Sawyer and his mother. Buz's father is dead. Buz joined the air force and went away last winter. Mrs. Sawyer said he lied about how old he was so he could go and fly planes. Mrs. Sawyer was mad about that. We're waiting for Buz to come back soon. Then, next to Buz is number seven where my friend Billy Batson lives with his mother. His father is at the war.

At number nine, the last in the row, there's Lenny Lipshitz and the Lipshitzes. Lenny's father is a rag man. A rag and bone and junk man. He has a horse with a bent back that pulls an old creaky wagon. He drives around all day, really slow in the wagon. Every little while he calls out something that means rags, bones, junk. He sits up there on his wagon half full of bedsprings and bottles and paper and bones and he's not sitting up straight. He looks like he's asleep.

Lenny Lipshitz has a face that makes you think he's lying all the time. I guess it's because he never looks right at you when he says something to you. He always looks away over your shoulder or down at your shoes when he talks. And his mouth acts funny when it tries to say the words. His mouth acts like it doesn't want to say the words it's saying.

And his cheeks go up a bit like your cheeks do when you stub your toe or you get your fingers caught in a door.

One day, at school, Lenny showed me a game called pennies in the pot. You dig a hole with your heel in the dirt. That's the pot. Then from three long steps away you each throw a penny and try to get it in or near the pot. Whoever is in, or closest, gets a turn shoving the other penny with his finger. If he gets it in he keeps both pennies. If he doesn't, it's the other guy's turn.

We played quite a while and I lost every time.

I was starting to run out of pennies when along came Miss Gilhooly, our art teacher. She was HORRIFIED and said that what we were doing was gambling and that gambling was evil and that we should give all the money back and get off the path of sin and wrong.

In my pocket I had three cents left.

"How much did you have before you started this GAMBLING?" Miss Gilhooly said. She had a look of great sadness on her face. She was looking at me like I was someone who just got a horrible disease and was going to get sent to a leper colony or to the Island of the Damned, like in the comics. I showed her the three cents I had left.

I looked straight into her eyes and said I had twenty cents when we started.

"Then Lenny," she said, "you'll give Martin back seventeen cents and never, never GAMBLE again!"

"But," Lenny said, "it wasn't seventeen cents, it was only ten cents. I won only ten cents from him!"

Lenny was looking down at Miss Gilhooly's big shoes and then up over her shoulder at the Union Jack flying over York Street School and his mouth was acting funny and his face was in pain.

"You're lying, Lenny," Miss Gilhooly said very quietly. "Now, you'll give Martin back his seventeen cents immediately or we go to the principal."

Of course, Lenny didn't want to go to the principal and

get tortured and maybe executed so he gave over the seventeen cents.

On my way home going past Provost's candy store I remembered something awful.

That morning I had two dimes that I found in the gutter just outside our house and I spent seven cents of it on a big Crispy Crunch chocolate bar and got a toothache for a while chewing away on the whole thing on my way to school.

So I really had only thirteen cents when I started GAMBLING.

Lennie was not lying. I was the liar.

I told my granny about it. She told me I have the kind of beautiful face that people will always want to believe. People want to believe what a beautiful face says.

And nobody will ever want to believe what Lenny Lipshitz says.

"Does that mean I always have to tell the truth?" I asked my granny.

"Yes," she said. "Telling the truth is best."

Then she said that I was a beautiful, beautiful boy and I'd have to learn to live with that the rest of my born days.

While I'm waiting for my mother and Phil to come back from the bank, I'm looking through my pile of *National Geographic* magazines — the ones that my granny used to bring over when she was finished reading them.

My favorite is the one about the Aztecs, the Nahuatl people of Mexico long, long ago. The Aztecs, every spring, would take the most beautiful boy of the tribe and give him presents and wonderful food and expensive clothes and money and parties with beautiful girls and music and rub him with oil and give him a crown and have a big parade for him and then at the end of it they would stretch his beautiful naked body across a golden altar and the priests would hold him down stretched out on his back as far as they could stretch him while everybody watched and prayed and with a silver knife they would cut out his heart and lift it up to give to the gods. So the crops would grow.

There was a colored painting of the altar and the Aztec priests cutting out the heart of the beautiful boy.

The knife and the blood.

4

Mr. George and the Choir Cat

MY MOTHER and Phil are back from the bank. Phil is howling and acting up. My mother gives me a whole dollar.

"Go up to Lefebvre's Shoe Market and get yourself a pair of running boots. They're ninety-nine cents. You can keep the cent left over. Those two women, two officials from the Assistance, seem to think you're not being brought up right. Neglected. You'd think they'd have the common decency to wait at least till after the funeral to come and load this on me. Bunch of busybodies."

My mother sits on the chesterfield. She's tired and her eyes are red. She's sitting on the part where there's no spring sticking up through.

There's a baby in her belly that's going to come out soon.

I walk up Cobourg Street past Heney Park on my way to sing in the Protestant choir. Billy Batson is with me. We're both supposed to be the summer boys in the choir.

We take the places of some of the regular boys who go away from Lowertown all summer to their uncles' farms or to their shacks and cabins along the rivers.

We're supposed to be Mr. Skippy Skidmore's summer boys.

Mr. Skippy Skidmore is our music teacher and choir master at York Street School. While I was singing in the school choir Mr. Skippy came right over and stood beside me and put his hands in my curly hair and put his ear down close to my mouth and listened to just me while practically the whole school was singing in the gym. We were singing "God Save the King" or some song like that.

Billy said Mr. Skippy did the same to him.

Billy Batson makes me laugh. He has the same name as the boy in the comic books who can change into Captain Marvel.

In the comics, a homeless orphan called Billy Batson meets a wizard who gives him a magic word to say. The word is SHAZAM!

S is for Solomon equals wisdom
H is for Hercules equals strength
A is for Atlas equals stamina
Z is for Zeus equals power and leadership
A is for Achilles equals courage
and
M is for Mercury equals speed.

The homeless orphan Billy Batson says SHAZAM! and then there's a picture that says BOOM! and Billy changes into Captain Marvel who looks a lot like Fred MacMurray, the movie star, except for his clothes. Captain Marvel has a tight red suit on with a yellow belt, yellow cuffs, yellow boots and a white cape with yellow trim.

And on his chest is a yellow lightning bolt.

When my friend Billy sees danger or needs help or is afraid or wants to help somebody in trouble or gets into a fight on Angel Square on the way to school or gets excited about something he says the word SHAZAM! and shuts his eyes and waits.

Of course, nothing happens. Nothing goes BOOM! and he doesn't change into Captain Marvel, but he says the word gives him supernatural powers and makes his brain swell up like Captain Marvel's chest.

We walk up Cobourg Street past Heney Park where last winter the little boy got run over by a coal truck after he slid on his cardboard sleigh down off the hill onto Clarence Street.

Then we stop to look in Radmore's pet shop window, the filthy window on Rideau Street, at the kittens and puppies and rabbits in there. This is where they got Cheap, my cat, last year for my birthday.

I am thinking about how, after Mr. Skippy listened to my voice and choir was over and I went to math class, our math teacher, Ketchy Balls, gave me a piece of paper with a note written that said I was supposed to come to St.

Alban's Church when the summer holidays started and sing in the choir there. The note was from Mr. S. Skidmore. Did the S. stand for Skippy?

After Ketchy Balls gave me the note he hit me on the legs with his secret stick.

He keeps a stick shoved up the sleeve of his coat. If a boy (never a girl) is doing something else instead of doing his math work, Ketchy Balls reaches into his secret sleeve and whips out the stick and stings him across the bare legs with it.

While I was trying to read the note (Mr. Skippy wasn't a very good writer), Ketchy Balls whipped out his stick and cut a red mark on my leg.

"You're supposed to be working on your math work right now, not reading notes from people!" said Ketchy Balls.

Everybody hates Ketchy Balls. One day last winter Killer Bodnoff hit him on the back of the head with an ice ball and knocked his hat off at recess. That afternoon Ketchy Balls tried to find out who did it but nobody would tell so all the boys in the room got the strap. What a man Ketchy Balls is.

Billy and me, we walk down Rideau Street past Imbro's Restaurant where everybody's in there munching on spaghetti and meat sauce and licking up delicious ice cream sundaes.

Past the public library where Billy always goes to get books to read.

I don't go there very often to get books. I read mostly

Granny's old *National Geographic* magazines or comics or the Ottawa *Journal*.

I'm a very good reader. I could even read before I went to school. My granny taught me.

The first thing I read was what was written on lots of our knives and forks and spoons in our kitchen drawer:

CHATEAU LAURIER HOTEL

Billy and me, we pass by the Little Theatre and up King Edward Avenue into Sandy Hill. Playing at the Little Theatre is *Road to Morocco* with my favorite singer Bing Crosby and his stupid friend named Bob Hope. Bob Hope is supposed to be funny but he isn't. Bing gets to sing "Moonlight Becomes You" to the beautiful Dorothy Lamour. I saw it and tell Billy all about it. I tell him about what Dorothy Lamour was wearing.

"She was wearing only half of a tight nightgown with a split all the way up the side and she had a big beautiful flower in her hair," I tell Billy.

"SHAZAM!" says Billy.

To get to choir you go down the back wooden steps of the church and in. Then you go to the basement. Ten stairs to the dark landing. Then turn right in the dark and go down five more. Then into the light of the choir hall.

Mr. Skippy is right there.

"Well!" he says. "We're here, are we? Martin and Billy. My two new summer boys. Well. Welcome. You know you get paid, don't you? Twenty-five cents for practicing three times a week? Not twenty-five cents for each practice but twenty-five cents for *three* practices. And twenty-five cents for Sunday service and *another* twenty-five cents for Evensong! That's how much per week? Of course! It's seventy-five cents a week. For singing! A king's ransom, don't you think? Now, if you're late for choir you get docked one cent a minute for every minute you're late. Now, you'll notice that these steps you just came down are made of wood. Some of them creak! If you're late for choir you're going to wish the steps didn't creak. Especially step number nine!"

He winks at a big man standing against the wall with an army uniform on. There are about ten other boys around the hall.

"Right, Mr. George?"

"Right you are, Mr. Skippy," says the man.

"Yes," says Mr. Skippy, "number nine squeaks the loudest. If you can remember, it's good to skip that step. Go from step number eight right over nine onto the landing. Don't thump on the landing. Then tippy-toe the last five and peek around into the choir hall before you come in. If Mr. Skippy has his back turned you can slip into your place which is right here. Yes, you may call me Mr. Skippy. Then when Mr. Skippy turns around from the piano and faces the choir and raises his hand to conduct the singing maybe he won't notice. But he sometimes does! And then Mr. Skippy might say this: 'A miracle! A boy is invisible and only seconds later, he's *visible*! How can this be possible? An empty bench becomes an occupied bench! Oh, this modern world! What will they think of next! Sing well, my summer boys!'"

Mr. Skippy is called Skippy because of his crippled foot. His ankle is really skinny. It's like a broom handle almost. And his foot is sort of like a slipper. Floppy like a leather slipper. When he walks, his foot slaps down on the floor with a whack.

Whack-a-whack, whack-a-whack, here comes Mr. Skippy Skidmore.

But the best thing Mr. Skippy does with his foot is when he's conducting the choir. He slaps his foot on the floor to keep time. You always know the beat when you're singing hymns because of Mr. Skippy's foot.

"O God our help in ages past
Our SLAP in SLAP to SLAP..."

We practice some hymns and then there's a choir recess and then we sing some more.

All the time we're singing, Mr. George is standing against the wall with his hands in his pockets, looking at us. He's got thick glasses on and sometimes it looks like he has more than two eyes. He's got reddish brown hair and a small mouth and his bottom teeth are further out than his top teeth. He's got a big chest and a big bum but a really narrow waist. Near the end of the practice he looks at me for a long time and then he winks.

While we're still singing he goes over to a big soft chair and looks into the chair. Suddenly I notice there's a big beautiful black cat sleeping in there. The choir cat. Mr.

George leans over and pets the beautiful cat once. Then he goes into the other part of the choir hall where there's a sort of kitchen and comes back out with a pair of big scissors.

He lifts a long white cape from the back of the chair but the cat's sleeping on the end of the cape.

Mr. George takes the scissors and cuts off the end of the cape that the cat is sleeping on so he can get the cape off the chair without bothering the cat! Lucky cat!

Then he puts on the cape, waves to all the boys and the last we all see is the cape going out the door with the end cut off of it, and then we hear step number nine do a heavy squeak.

"Amen!" sings the choir, and the practice is over.

Just before he disappeared out the door, Mr. George gave another big wink from behind his thick glasses.

The wink was right at me again.

5

The Ideal Father

WALKING HOME from choir practice with Billy
Batson. Going by the Little Theatre again we see
the sign about the movie *Road to Morocco* starring Bing
Crosby. I sing some of my favorite songs to Billy like Bing
Crosby sings in the movie to Dorothy Lamour:
"Moonlight becomes you...It goes with your hair...You
certainly know the right things to wear..."

Billy says did I see Mr. George at choir cut his cape so
the beautiful choir cat wouldn't have to disturb himself?

Yes. I saw. Everybody saw.

What kind of a person would do that?

A very kind, considerate person, we guess.

I tell Billy about how my father once yanked up his
scarf my cat Cheap was sleeping on on the bed and sent
Cheap flying against the wall.

What kind of a person would do that?

A mean, cruel person, we guess.

Billy starts telling me again about his father. Billy's

father went away to the war more than five years ago and should be home soon now that the war's almost over.

Billy loves his father. He says his father was always bringing him presents and taking him places — hardware stores and lumber yards where they'd go to get stuff and bring it all home and build all kinds of things. And how they always dug in their garden together all the time.

And how they'd find worms there and put them in a can with some moss and put them in the icebox and save them until they had a chance to go down to the Ottawa River near the Rideau Falls at night and catch a bunch of catfish and take them home and his mother would cook them and they'd sit down together and have a big catfish feast...

We pass by Imbro's Restaurant again and stop for a while and watch through the window people gobbling ice cream sundaes. In one of the booths along the side I think I see the back of Mr. George's head. Or maybe it's not.

On the corner of Rideau and Augusta Street there's a sign nailed to the telephone pole:

Street Dance: honouring 20 repats recently
arrived on the *Isle de France*;
an interesting evening of foxtrot, waltzes,
spot dances and old time dances,
door prizes and *new* features e.g.
"fat woman's race!"
Public address system set up.
Public is cordially invited to attend.

37

We can hear the music coming out of the public address system. We go down there to see if we can see the fat ladies have their race but it's too late, it's over.

There's soldiers and girls dancing and kids running around and people laughing and eating.

The horse that pulls a chip wagon is standing there asleep through all the racket.

There's an Ottawa *Journal* lying on a bench.

I pick it up on the way by.

I read some of the stuff in there to Billy as we walk home.

Wife butcher-knifes Vet husband to death over uncooked supper: son, Henry, 10 years old

and

Lady with 27 cats in her bed. Husband sleeps in the kitchen.

and

Take wonderful Lux toilet soap whipped cream lather facials daily like Veronica Lake does. Soon your Romance complexion will charm men's hearts!

There's a picture of Veronica Lake with her beautiful hair covering one eye. I show the picture to Billy.

"SHAZAM!" says Billy.

It's going to be dark soon.

They're playing football on Heney Street beside the park. There are two Christian Brothers from Brebeuf school playing with their long black dresses on. One

Brother lifts his skirts with one hand and holds the football out in front of himself with the other hand and kicks the football. It goes so high above Heney Park it almost disappears. You can see the Brother's underpants when he kicks.

It's the other Brother's turn. He tries to kick but his leg goes higher than the ball. He's not a very good kicker. His leg gets tangled up in his dress and he falls over.

All the kids around laugh.

On Papineau Street Horseball's big family is spilling out of the windows.

At my place, number three Papineau, I can hear shouting. Fighting. Arguing.

Billy's looking at me funny. What's he thinking? Is he thinking about his ideal father?

When my parents fight, my twin brother, Phil, howls and roars.

Phil can't talk. Phil can't think. He can't even eat right. His food is always all over the place. He can't go to the toilet on his own. Except in his diapers that my mother changes on him every morning and every night. And he's always hurting himself. Somebody has to be there all the time.

When he's happy he likes to run around in a circle. Or he likes to wag his head. He holds on to the end of his iron bed and throws his head, wags his head back and forward in a sort of a circle, looks at the floor, the wall, the ceiling and the floor again except his eyes are closed, again and again and again.

I ask Billy if he wants to do something. Trade comics maybe, go to his place maybe.

No, he can't. Billy never invites me to his place. I've never been inside number seven Papineau. I've been at Horseball's house many times even though you have to stand up against the wall it's so crowded in there.

And everybody's been in Buz Sawyer's place. Buz was always inviting everybody over — giving treats and telling stories.

And I've been in Lenny Lipshitz's house, number nine Papineau. The time I went over to give him back the money from the GAMBLING.

His mother gave me some gefilte fish. I didn't like it but I didn't say anything.

Lenny said he really liked gefilte fish but I didn't believe him.

But I've never been in Billy Batson's house. My mother told me once that she thought Mrs. Batson was ashamed of something.

Or was hiding something. I forget which.

I'd like to see a picture of this ideal father he has.

And so, in my place, Martin O'Boy's, I have to go. There's yelling and hollering.

My brother Phil is probably under the bed barking like a dog.

6

Cheap and the Perfect Twin

I'M SITTING on the edge of my mother's bed. My father slammed out of the house after the fight. Phil's asleep in our room.

My mother gets me to feel the baby inside kicking. *Kick, kick.* Like a little fist punching under a soft blanket. *Kick.* He wants to get out. Let me out. I want to be in the world!

I tell my mother about the fat ladies' race at the street dance.

"My God, what will they think of next! Those parties are getting out of hand. What self-respecting woman would go in a thing like that? All that flab jiggling and flopping and bouncing around!"

My mother tells me about the two ladies the other day. The ketchup lady and the turkey lady.

"They think we're not taking proper care of you. They said that at school last winter you weren't dressed warm enough with just your big sweater and that you were caught GAMBLING and that you planned some violent summer activity in art class and they saw your rubbers instead of shoes. You'll go first thing in the morning to get the shoes. I gave you the dollar."

Cheap comes in and jumps on the bed with us. He looks sad with his missing ear.

I'm wondering if he worries about anything like I do. Does he ever wonder about anything? Or does he just wait around for something to come along?

"You're the perfect one," my mother says, stroking my head. "You can't be causing trouble now, can you, sweetheart? Phil is trouble enough, don't you think?"

Cheap is starting to purr. Getting comfortable.

The baby is kicking.

"You'll have to mind Phil tomorrow, you know."

"Why?"

"Granny's funeral. We have to go to the funeral."

"Why can't I go to Granny's funeral?"

"Because you have to mind Phil."

"Maybe Mrs. Batson or somebody could mind Phil."

"I couldn't ask her to do that. You can't ask anybody to do that."

"What about Horseball's mother or one of the older sisters? Maybe one of them."

"No, I couldn't. And don't call him Horseball. It's not nice. Call him by his real name. What's his proper name, anyway?"

"Horseball."

"No. His real name."

"Horace, I think. Something like Horace."

Back in my room I look at Phil there asleep in his bed. He looks so calm. I go in the bathroom and in the mirror there, I try to look like Phil.

I open my mouth wide like I'm howling and I make my eyes as big as I can and I pull my hair back hard until what I see in the mirror scares me.

Back in my bed, Cheap sleeps with me. Half on the pillow beside me.

I think I love Cheap. Do I?

I don't know if I love anybody else.

I sing "Moonlight Becomes You" to Cheap.

He wiggles his only ear. He likes Bing Crosby.

When I talk to Cheap he squeezes his eyes shut. And if he's on the bed, he pulls on the blanket with his claws — first the right paw, then the left. Just like you see kittens doing when they suck milk from their mother.

When I stop talking, he opens his eyes and looks at me and stops kneading his claws. His eyes are wide open. He's saying, "Talk to me some more. I like when you talk to me…"

My mother told me that when grown-up cats act like that it means they didn't get enough love when they were babies.

Soon I'll get Cheap some catnip. There's lots of it growing in Lenny Lipshitz's yard. Lenny's father told me that if I took any catnip out of the yard I'd have to pay ten cents for a handful but Lenny says never mind paying, just go in the yard at night when the old man's asleep and steal it.

Cheap loves catnip. He rolls around in it and wrestles with it. His eyes get a crazy tilt in them and he looks like, if he could, he would sing a big musical number — something like Judy Garland in *Meet Me in St. Louis* when she sang "The Trolley Song."

7

New Shoes

IT WILL be hot today. I'll have to go for ice after I get home with the new shoes.

I walk up Clarence Street past the Lee Kung Laundry. Steam is coming out the door all the time. Smells like boiled potatoes.

It's garbage day on Clarence Street. I walk by the garbage wagon. The horses are covered with horse flies and the wagon and the garbage men are covered with garbage flies. The guy throwing the cans up to the guy on top of the wagon is looking at the rubbers tied on with elastics I'm wearing instead of shoes.

"Great lookin' pair of special kind of shoes ya have there!" he says. And he laughs a big laugh.

A large juicy fly flies into his mouth. Good.

Mr. Lipshitz's horse clops by pulling Mr. Lipshitz and some bedsprings and bottles and paper and rags and bones. Mr. Lipshitz looks like he's asleep.

At the corner of Clarence and Dalhoozie is Lefebvre

Shoe Market. From here up Dalhoozie Street I can see the Français theater. Playing is *Hold That Ghost* starring Abbott and Costello. It's about a haunted castle. Costello is sitting at a table and a candle on the table starts to move. Also, a wall turns around and he disappears.

In Lefebvre's Shoe Market there's a party. Somebody came home from the war. There's sandwiches and ice cream and Kik cola and beer and whiskey.

The sign in the window says:

> CORK-SOLED RUNNERS —
> 99 CENTS!

A man who is pretty drunk laughs at my rubbers, pulls off the elastics, shoots the elastics at another man and a girl eating sandwiches.

Across the store in the back part some people are singing a French song that's something like "Row, Row, Row Your Boat" and one big woman is choking she's laughing so much.

My big toe is sticking through a hole in my right sock.

"That's nice and cool, eh, for a hot summer day! Air conditioning! The latest thing! Hey, look at this, everyone! Air conditioning! The latest thing!"

He gets a pair of the cork-soled runners out of a pile of them in a bin. He puts them both on me and ties them too tight. They seem to be way too long for my feet.

"Perfect!" he says and stands up, staggering backwards a bit. "A perfect fit!"

"I think they're too big," I say. He bends down and feels for my toes in the shoe. He pulls the shoe hard from the back so that my foot pushes into the front of the shoe. He feels my toes.

"See! There's your toes, right there where they should be. A perfect fit!"

"I think they're too big," I say.

"Tell you what. You go out and take a walk around the block. Try them out. You'll see. They fit! And look how nice and brand new they look! Go ahead, try them out. And, hey, don't forget to come back and give me the ninety-nine cents!"

I leave the store and walk up Dalhoozie Street past the Français theater and around the block.

These shoes are so long they flap when I walk. Each step slaps the sidewalk. Something like Mr. Skippy Skidmore only twice as bad.

Slap, flap, flap, slap!

People on the sidewalk are looking at me and my shoes and whispering to each other.

I go back into Lefebvre's Shoe Market.

I can't find the man who told me to go out and walk around the block and try out the shoes.

The party is not as loud now. Most of the people are gone. A short woman with a big chest and lots of teeth comes over. I explain to her about the shoes.

"Did you pay for the shoes?" she says.

Should I lie? Should I lie, Granny? I could lie. I could say yes I paid for the shoes and then I could keep the dollar and nobody would know. Better not. Granny might be watching.

"No," I say, looking right at her. "No, I didn't."

"You owe ninety-nine cents," she says.

I give her the dollar. She gives me back one cent.

"Thank you, dear," she says. "Come back again!"

"But these shoes don't fit," I say. "They're too big, too long."

"We can't change them now. You already wore them outside. Look at the bottoms. They're all scuffed. I can't sell those shoes to somebody else. We don't sell *used shoes* here at Lefebvre's Shoe Market — serving Ottawa since 1910!"

"But they're so big!" I say. "They go slap, flap."

"Too bad. Who told you to walk around outside in these shoes?"

"A man. A man who works here."

"Nobody who works here would do that. It must have been just a joke. There was a little party here. I'll tell you what. I'll give you a discount. How's that? Okay? Mmm?"

She goes into the till and gives me a dime.

"There," she says. "Shoes on sale specially for a handsome sweet boy like you! Bye-bye!"

I decide to go home by St. Patrick Street because I don't want the garbage men who laughed at my rubbers to see my shoes.

Flap, slap, slap, flap — all the way down St. Patrick Street.

8

Trap Door Spider

MY MOTHER'S dressed up. She's got a purple hat on and a purple silky scarf and purple flat shoes. Her belly's pretty big so her black dress with the purple collar doesn't fit right. She keeps pulling down on it. I can smell the perfume she put on her silky scarf and behind her ears and on her wrists.

I know what kind of perfume it is. It's Blue Grass Eau de Parfum. She keeps it in a special drawer in her bureau with her silky scarf and some rings and necklaces. The drawer I'm not supposed to look in.

Once, when nobody was around, I sprayed Phil with the Blue Grass Eau de Parfum. He hated it and he started howling. I guess he'd rather smell the way he usually smells.

My mother never gets dressed up.

Because she never goes anywhere.

My father's standing at the door smoking cigarettes. He's waiting. They're not fighting for a change. My father has his good hat on and his shoes are shined. He has on the suit he wears to work all the time but a different tie.

My mother's crying a little bit.

My father looks at my new runners with the cork soles. "Nice shoes ya got," he says. "Too bad they don't fit."

My mother's always late. They fight about that a lot. Or she stays in the bathroom too long. They fight about that a lot too. Or she burns the supper. Or she doesn't order the right kind of groceries at Peter Devine's on the market.

My father gets pretty mad a lot.

But he never hits. He told me his father used to beat him with a whip and that's why he never hits us. And he never will.

But he sure can yell and curse and call you names and break stuff and throw chairs around and slam doors and boot basins and things around the house. One time he threw his pisspot down the stairs. Lucky there wasn't too much in it. He keeps the pisspot beside the bed because my mother stays in the bathroom so long sometimes that he can't wait.

Once when she was in there for about an hour he yelled at the door, "What are ya doin'? Washin' yerself with a Q-tip?"

Washing your whole body with a Q-tip? A little stick with cotton batting on the end that you use to clean out your ears?

He makes me laugh sometimes, my father does. In a cruel sort of way.

Once, when my mother was in the bathroom for so

long and he was pounding on the door with his fist so that the door was rattling and shaking, he shouted, "Yer gonna be sorry because I'm tellin' ya fer the last time I can't wait so don't blame me fer what's goin' to happen!"

Then he went and got a straw and a glass of water from the kitchen and he filled his mouth with water and poked the straw through the keyhole of the bathroom door and blew the stream of water into the bathroom.

My mother was screaming, "You monster!" and he was shouting, "I told ya, I told ya you'd be sorry! A man can't wait forever on a woman to get out of the bathroom. He'll do anything, a man will, to empty out his bladder!"

They're gone on the streetcar to the funeral. First St. Brigid's Church, then to Notre Dame Cemetery.

To put Granny in the ground. That's what my father said. "We're gonna put Granny in the ground."

Minding Phil should be easy. He's upstairs wagging his head.

I can read the Ottawa *Journal* for a while in peace and quiet. In the paper there's a picture of a can of Spam the same as we have in our icebox. The paper says that the Allied troops in the Second World War which is nearly over ate 250 million cans of Spam so far.

I go to the icebox and make myself a Spam sandwich with Pan Dandy bread. The label on the can says: *chopped pork shoulder meat with ham, salt, water, sugar and sodium nitrate.*

I read everything that's written down anywhere. I can't help it. My granny told me to always read everything. She said everything you see that's written down, "You read it!"

While I'm eating the Spam sandwich I'm thinking of my friend Buz Sawyer who lied about his age so he could go to the war and fly airplanes.

Maybe he's having a Spam sandwich right now too. Me and Buz. I hope he's home soon.

We miss him. He always protected us. Me and Billy.

I put down the Ottawa *Journal* and go and get one of Granny's *National Geographic* magazines out of the cellar.

The one I'm reading is about spiders.

There's a big colored picture of a special spider called a trap door spider.

Trap door spiders dig tube-like burrows in the ground which they seal with a hinged lid or trap door. The spider holds the trap shut with its fangs until it senses vibrations made by passing prey. Then the spider rushes out, seizes the victim, and drags it into the burrow.

Reading this I imagine being the victim.

The trap door spider has multiple (8) eyes, 2 small jaws and fangs. It paralyzes its prey then rubs and crushes its victim. Each leg is divided in seven segments. Cephalothorax and abdomen are separated by a narrow "waist" or pedicle.

I hold the picture of the spider up close and stare into its eyes. I'm waiting for the eight legs to scurry out and grab me. Seize me, drag me away, paralyze me, rub me, crush me.

It's scaring me but I can't look away.

Billy Batson's at the door. And Phil is coming down-stairs. I let Billy in. He sees Phil. Billy's a bit afraid of Phil.

"SHAZAM!" says Billy and shuts his eyes. He's pre-tending to change into Captain Marvel in case Phil starts acting up.

I show Billy the *National Geographic* about the trap door spider. I hold the big colored picture of the spider up to Billy's face and try to hypnotize him. Phil's trying to bang on the magazine and maybe rip the pages. It's no use. You can't do anything when Phil's around. I put away the magazine and get the rubber ball that my grampa used to bounce off his head before he went to the Home.

We sit on the floor and roll the ball around to keep Phil busy. The ball rolls in behind Phil's diaper pail in the corner. The pail has a big dent in it half the size of the pail.

"See where my father kicked the pail?" I tell Billy. "My father calls the pail Old Faithful. I know what he means by that. Old Faithful is a geyser in a big park somewhere that shoots hot water up in the air once a day — never fails. I read about it in the *National Geographic*."

My mother and father were arguing and fighting about money. There was no money to pay the milkman. Phil was howling. Phil's full dirty diaper pail was there on the floor. My father kicked it so hard that the water and diapers and everything else in the pail flew right up to the ceiling like an explosion of an underground geyser.

"Right up to the ceiling," says Billy, looking up at the

stain.

Billy's keeping an eye on Phil. Phil can be pretty mean sometimes — try to push you downstairs maybe, or hit you with a stick or try to throw a rock at you.

Billy's saying his father never did anything like kick Old Faithful. Billy's father would never yell at him or make fun of him in front of people.

Once, in the winter, we were chopping ice in front of our door to get a big puddle of ice water to run out onto the street. My father and me, chopping ice together. Then along comes Billy with his ax to help out and after we chopped for a while my father all of a sudden says I'm not chopping right and that Billy's a lot better at chopping than I am and a better worker than me and that I am just a useless tool is what I am.

A useless tool.

Billy tells me his father has a nice soft voice and never yells and smells really nice. He says he remembers how nice his father smells. He smells like leather or sweet tobacco from his pipe. Or shaving soap. My father smells sometimes of Aqua Velva.

Aqua Velva is stuff in a bottle that stings your face after you shave. Once, while I was watching my father shave, I saw him take a big drink out of his Aqua Velva bottle.

Billy's lucky to have a father like he has.

We guess he'll be home soon, now that the war's almost over. Him and Buz.

There's nothing to do but mind Phil.

We read stuff to him out of the Ottawa *Journal*.

There's a picture of a cow advertising milk and ice cream. The cow is saying, "If it's Borden's, it's got to be good!" We read that to Phil trying to sound like the cow. Phil doesn't like it. He starts howling. Then we read him, "Kellogg's Rice Krispies go snap crackle and pop!"

He howls some more.

To calm him down we turn on the radio and try and get the programs. The ones my mother listens to in the afternoon.

"Road of Life," then "Ma Perkins," then "Pepper Young's Family," then "Right to Happiness." The programs calm Phil down. It's the music and the quiet talking.

Cheap comes in the room yawning.

The sun is slanting in the window.

Billy goes home.

Now my mother and father are at the door.

They are quiet. Not fighting.

Granny's in the ground now.

9

"Who's Coming to Me!"

O N A SIGN near the door of the Protestant church there's the story of who St. Alban was. I read it again. I read it each time I come to choir practice, even though I've read it before. I can't help it. The sign tells the story of how St. Alban was the first Christian martyr in Britain.

A martyr is somebody who gives up his life for other people. Like the beautiful Aztec boy with his heart ripped out, I guess.

There was a priest on the run from the Romans because it was the sentence of death if you were caught being a Christian. In this modern world you'd get fried in the electric chair — in old Sparky like in *Crime Does Not Pay* comics which my mother doesn't want me to read or *Sheena the Jungle Girl* because Sheena never has very many clothes on. Anyway, you'd get scourged and beheaded. Scourged means whipped with whips until your skin falls off.

This priest talked Alban, who was a Roman soldier,

into being a Christian. One night the soldiers came looking for the priest on the run and Alban hid the priest
under some hay and put on his robes and gave himself up
to the soldiers and said *he* was the priest.

Then the soldiers scourged him and just so he'd never
do that again they beheaded him.

That's how you get to be St. Alban.

Into the church. Now the ten stairs to the dark landing. I'm late. I can hear the singing. Skip stair number
nine. Hang on to the railing that you can't quite get your
fingers all the way around. Hop to the landing. Then turn
right in the dark and go down five more.

But wait, there's somebody with me on the landing.

"Sh!" he says. "You're late." Big hands on me. He lifts
me down the five stairs to the doorway to the choir hall.
He looks out.

"Okay!" he says. "All clear. Go!"

It's Mr. George.

Mr. Skippy's back is turned. I slip into my place and
pick up my hymn book and start singing.

Mr. Skippy turns for the "Amen!"

"A miracle!" Mr. Skippy says. "A boy is invisible and
only seconds later, he's visible! How can this be possible?
An empty bench becomes an occupied bench. Oh, this
modern world! What will they think of next! Sing well, my
summer boy!"

Everybody's smiling.

Mr. George takes over the piano. Mr. George is the
summer piano and organ player.

At choir recess Mr. George has a game he plays with the younger boys. We move all the chairs and benches back. He pretends there's a line across the middle of the room. The older boys go outside and sneak cigarettes.

Mr. George gets on one side of the line and he stretches out his long arms. He says he's the goalie. He stretches, bends out his long legs — there's something funny about his legs, the way they are joined — and stretches out his long arms and his big hands and he moves back and forward across the line.

We can only go one at a time. We run and try to get by him. We're like a soccer ball trying to get past Mr. George, the goalie. He moves back and forward, back and forward. His face is there, the thick glasses, the brown red hair down his cheeks, his bottom teeth over.

The boys, one at a time.

"Five cents if you get by me! Five cents if you get by me and touch the wall! Line up! Everybody gets a turn."

Mr. George's eyes are burning behind his thick glasses and his red brown hair is flickering in the choir-room lights above.

The first boy goes. He runs at Mr. George and then ducks at the last minute under Mr. George's arm and makes it to the wall. Mr. George fishes into the pocket of his army pants and comes out with a nickel and flips it back to the wall without looking. He never takes his eyes off us. With the thick glasses and the lights above he has many eyes. He's hypnotizing us.

The boy picks up the nickel after it bounces off the

wall. He laughs and jumps up and down and spits on the nickel and puts it in his pocket and pats his pocket.

"This is easy!" shouts the boy. "I want to try again!"

"No, no," says Mr. George. "You have to go to the end of the line. Everybody has a turn! Who's next? Come on. Let's go!"

The next boy runs up. He's like a little fish. He dives between Mr. George's jointed legs and escapes to the wall. Everybody cheers. Mr. George flips another nickel over his shoulder.

"Next boy! Next boy! Hurry! Hurry! Next boy! Who's coming to me!"

Billy is next. He steps up. "SHAZAM!" says Billy. BOOM! He flashes around the end of Mr. George's hand, quick as Captain Marvel. Five cents please.

I'm the next boy.

I'm thinking of when I play soccer with a tennis ball. To score a goal I push the ball to my left, then I pretend I'm cutting to the right and then I keep to the left and kick the ball into the net.

I run toward Mr. George and move to the left and then pretend to go to the right. Mr. George moves over and for a minute I think I've got him, but my shoes...

My shoes, my Lefebvre's Shoe Market special, on sale, way too big cork-soled runners tangle me up and I can't change back to my left and he grabs me and pulls me into him and squeezes me. I'm squirming and I'm mad and trying to get away because I don't want to be the first one caught.

I hate to be no good at something.

I can feel his rough whiskers on my neck and his hot breath in my ear.

But now I feel his arms relax and start to let go and I hear him shouting, "He's getting away! He's getting away!" and he lets me slip away and I'm to the wall.

I hear the coin hit the wall. It sounds a little different. Heavier. I pick it up. It's not a nickel.

It's a whole quarter!

10

A Crazy Man

THERE'S something happening, something bad happening on Papineau Street. It's the middle of the night and everybody's up — even Phil. My father's pulling on his pants and my mother's wrapped in her big nightgown that's like a big white towel with a belt tied over the top of her belly. I get some clothes on Phil and we go out into the street.

There's a big crowd. There's two policemen with flashlights talking to Mrs. Batson.

Billy's standing across the street.

"Somebody came in our house and now he's in there and he won't come out!"

Billy's scared. He's not saying SHAZAM. He's shaking. The police are shining flashlights in the Batsons' windows.

The street is filling up. A police wagon drives up. Ringing his bell. A whole lot of Horseball Laflamme's big family are out watching. Maybe all of them. Lenny

Lipshitz is there and his mother. And here comes his father. See how wide awake he is! And Mrs. Sawyer is now talking to Mrs. Batson. Now she puts her arms around her and Mrs. Batson puts her head on her shoulder and sobs.

There's a whole lot of people from Cobourg Street and from down on Augusta and even from across Angel Square maybe.

It's almost like a street dance or a party.

"A crazy man is in the Batsons' house!"

"He tried to kill the Batsons!"

"He pounded and pounded on the door and then he broke the door because they wouldn't let him in."

"Who is he?"

"We don't know."

"Why is he crazy? What's the matter with him? Is it because of the war? Is he a soldier?"

"No, he wasn't in uniform. At least not a vet's uniform."

"Looked like whites. Like hospital clothes."

"Maybe he's from the loony bin."

"The nut house."

"There's lots of them running around."

"I think it's because of the war."

"The war is almost over except for those Japanese!"

"Do you think they'll ever give up?"

"It's just a matter of time."

"I'll believe it when I see it."

Two policemen push in the door. There's something holding it shut but they get it open and go in with their flashlights and their sticks.

One policeman's got a gun.

There's a lot of shouting. The policemen come out holding a man in white clothes. The man looks wild. He's a short man with a big head. There's blood on his knuckles and his cheek is bleeding.

"The policeman hit him with his stick right in the face!"

The wagon shines a searchlight on the man. They take him to the wagon. His feet are hardly touching the road. He glares at Billy on the way by. His face is full of something. Terror. And there's something wrong with one of his eyes. He has a glass eye.

"He's terrified!"

"He's crazy!"

"He's nutty as a fruitcake!"

"He's a raving lunatic!"

"He's not all there!"

"He's got a screw loose!"

"Who is he, anyway?"

The bell on the wagon is ringing. Phil is howling.

The policemen go in the house with Billy and Mrs. Batson and shut the door. You can see them in the living room talking quiet to Billy's mother. The wagon is gone.

Everybody's heading out. The party is over.

All the Laflammes go back in their place. How do they all fit in there?

There's hardly anybody around now. My father carries Phil into the house. My mother and Mrs. Sawyer are talking and shaking their heads. Then Mrs. Sawyer goes in and shuts her door quiet, so quiet. The lights are going out on Papineau Street.

My mother and I are left. We're standing in front of our step. She looks long at me. In my eyes. There's deep sadness in my mother's face.

"That man," she says to me, "is Billy Batson's father..."

Billy Batson's father!

11

Poor Billy

I WAKE UP yelling. Because of a horrible dream. I dreamt I woke up and I was just like Phil. I couldn't talk, I couldn't think, I couldn't go to the toilet, I couldn't catch a ball, I looked horrible in the mirror, like a fish, I had goobers in my nose, food hanging out of my mouth, yellow slime in the corner of my eyes, crooked teeth…and howling like a wounded animal…

In my dream I went outside. Phil was trying to fry an egg on the sidewalk.

Phil is talking. He's explaining science: "If the temperature were 95 degrees on a hot summer day like today and the cement was sufficiently new and smooth, the sand in the cement mix being of a fairly high percentage of minerals for conductivity, it is conceivable that one could literally fry an egg on the sidewalk…" The egg is sizzling away on the sidewalk. I'm trying to say "Phil" but my mouth doesn't work. Suddenly Phil crawls over like a crab and with huge jaws clamps on my leg… I'm pulling,

pulling away but I can't escape... I'm trying to kill Phil with a big iron bar...

While I'm waking up and yelling out of my dream I see Phil over in his bed, lying on his side, looking at me.

I get up, take Phil downstairs and have some snap crackle and pop and try to feed Phil some to help my mother but he spits most of it out and then tries to throw my bowl on the floor.

My mother is talking about Billy's father.

"Count your blessings," says my mother. "At least your father is in the category of *normal*. Sort of."

It's time for ice so I get my wagon out of the shed.

On the front step our enamel basin is lying upside down. My father probably kicked it out the door when he was leaving for work. He works for the Civil Service. He calls it the Silver Service. His office is in the big Connaught Building on Sussex Street. He calls it the Cannot Building.

The Cannot Building on Such and Such Street instead of Sussex Street.

He often boots around our enamel basin. He boots it downstairs, or into the cellar or out into the yard or up against the wall. There's not much enamel left on the basin and it's full of dents.

And sometimes he kicks Old Faithful but not so much because the dent in it is so big Old Faithful doesn't shoot up as high as it did the first time he booted it.

On the way up St. Patrick Street and over to St. Andrew I'm thinking what my mother said about Billy's father. How the Batsons moved in on Papineau Street about six years ago before the war and how she always thought there was something odd about Mrs. Batson's story about Mr. Batson being sent over before the war even started. And how she told Billy that his father was a war hero and how Billy then made up the rest of the stuff about what a great dad he was and how nice he was to everybody and all that about how they'd build things together and how nice he smelled and how kind he was.

Poor Billy.

They locked his daddy up in the loony bin because something happened to his brain and he started attacking people. Jumping out at strangers and chasing them.

On St. Andrew Street there's a lot of broken bottles and streamers and party hats lying around. They must have had another big street dance for the repats last night.

I wonder when Buz is coming. Soon, I hope.

Wait! Here comes Ketchy Balls! I hide behind a telephone post. He doesn't see me. He must live around here. I've never seen him in the summer. He looks different. He looks almost human. Almost like a real person. He hasn't got his suit on. Probably hasn't even got his stick with him. But you never know. He probably does have his stick with him. Hits kids all summer just for practice.

Once, in school, Ketchy Balls told me I couldn't go out for recess with the rest of the class because he wanted me to stay in and help him with a job he had to do. Ketchy Balls is not just a math work teacher. He's also a gymnasium teacher. The job we had to do was go into a storeroom and lock the door and blow up some basketballs and some soccer balls with a bicycle pump.

The pump was hard to push down even with two hands so he put his big hairy hand over my two hands and squeezed so hard while pushing down on the pump that he almost broke my fingers and tears came to my eyes and I yelled out.

"Don't be such a sissy!" he whispered to me and squeezed harder. "And don't you dare yell, or you'll get the secret stick!"

E.A.Bourque ICE/GLACE is one block away on St. Andrew. I can smell the wet sawdust from here.

I love it in the cool dark ice house.

I drag my wagon in there. You go in the office first. You give the dime to the man and get your ticket. There's always two men. They're drinking beer and talking about the war. They wish they could've gone but maybe next time.

Outside the office deep in the ice house I give my ticket to the man there. His head reminds me of my father's pisspot.

"Hi there, pretty boy," he says to me. "Where didja get the shoes?"

"At Lefebvre's Shoe Market," I say.

"What's wrong with them?" he says.

"Nothing's wrong with them," I say.

"They're too long, aren't they? Those feet, you look like a penguin."

"And your head reminds me of my father's pisspot," I whisper.

"What'd you say?"

"Nothing," I say.

"Pretty boy smart ass like you could get a slap in the ear!" he says and puts a block of ice on my wagon. It's smaller than it's supposed to be.

"If you hurry home with that there might be some left when you get there! Smart ass pretty boy!"

I pull the wagon down St. Andrew and over to St. Patrick and here's Billy come to meet me. He knows I always go for ice on this day. I'm trying to keep it in the shade. There's already water dripping out of my wagon, leaving a trail.

"My father says you could maybe fry a fried egg on the sidewalk today," I say to Billy. "It's going to be so hot."

"My father used to say that all the time too," says Billy.

I look at Billy. I'm going to say it to him. I do say it to him.

"Mrs. Sawyer told my mother that that man last night was your father."

Billy looks at me.

"SHAZAM!" Billy says. "Mrs. Sawyer tells lies."

"Who was that crazy man last night?"

"I don't know. Just some crazy crazy man, I guess."

There's a guy on the veranda of his little house on St. Patrick Street next door to Petigorsky Shoe Repair. He's got his dog. He pets the dog and he pets the dog and he rubs the dog's stomach and rolls the dog and he loves the dog.

Billy can't keep his eyes off the guy and his dog. They're

having so much fun together. They like each other so
much.

Billy wishes he was that dog.

12

Organ Pipes

WE'RE A LITTLE early, Billy and me, for choir.
Mr. George is taking five of us summer boys up to
the choir loft to see the organ pipes. The room is up over
the altar in the church where all the organ music comes
from. There's Billy and me and Dick Dork, Darce the Arse
and Dumb Doug.

Billy named these summer boys. We don't know what
their real names are.

We go up a steep staircase in back of the altar.

Mr. George opens the door to the loft with a key and
then I see him reach up and hang the key back on the nail.
High up on the side of the door jamb.

"This is out of bounds, my summer boys," says Mr.
George. "Nobody's allowed in this room unless they are
with me. Is that clear?"

In the room there are rows of pipes standing straight up
and down. At one end of the row they are as big and tall
as stove pipes. At the other end as thin and short as little

flutes. Each pipe has a wedged hole in it part way up like in a whistle. The top of each pipe is open. It has a sleeve that Mr. George can pull up or push down to make the pipe longer or shorter. That's the way he tunes the organ. To make sure the notes are right. If he makes the pipe just a tiny bit longer, then that one note is a tiny bit lower. If he taps the sleeve on top and makes the pipe a little bit shorter, then the note that pipe makes is a little bit higher.

Each key on the organ downstairs near the altar is attached to one of these pipes.

The pipes that are as big as stovepipes are the low notes. The tiny pipes at the other end are the high notes.

There's a step ladder here to change the tops of the big stovepipe notes, they're so high.

"Now you boys wait here and don't you dare touch anything! Just stand there and I'll be right back," says Mr. George. He goes out of the loft and shuts the door. Then the lights go out.

Soon Mr. George is down at the organ. You can see him sitting down there through the slats in the wall. Now tiny notes start coming out of the smallest pipes, the little whistles, lots of teeny, high notes running up and down like pretty water falls or teensy rain tinkling.

Now the bigger pipes start playing, like bugles and car horns and the factory whistle at the paper mill. And the noise in the nearly pitch dark room is starting to hurt our ears.

Now it gets louder, and the notes get lower now and the bigger pipes are blowing and sounding like bulls howling and trains whistling and I can see the shadows of the summer boys putting their hands over their ears. Now the biggest pipes start to pound and bellow and rumble like thunder and crash and roll and explode like earthquakes and volcanoes and the whole room is shaking and vibrating and shuddering and the low notes are coming up our legs and into our hearts and boiling into my brain until my whole body is shaking and I'm falling apart and the floor cracks open and the room comes tumbling down around us.

All of a sudden everything stops. The silence is ringing away.

I just stepped off a cliff into space.

The light goes on.

Mr. George opens the door.

"Wasn't that fun, my summer boys? Now, let's go down with Mr. Skippy and sing our brave little hearts out, shall we?"

13
The Show

A T THE FRANÇAIS theater today there's a big lineup to go and see *Double Indemnity* starring Billy's favorite actor, Fred MacMurray. We've already seen it. Fred MacMurray is Billy's favorite actor because he looks just like Captain Marvel. Or Captain Marvel looks like Fred MacMurray. Which is which?

"Captain Marvel has lived forever. He's immortal," says Billy. "So it must be that he came first. So you have to say that Fred MacMurray looks like Captain Marvel."

"How did he do that?" I say. "How do you get to look like somebody like Captain Marvel?"

"I guess you have to really try hard," says Billy.

Of course, Fred MacMurray doesn't wear a red suit with a yellow lightning bolt on the chest and a white cape with yellow trim and yellow boots.

Fred in *Double Indemnity* wears a suit just like my

father wears to go and work in the Silver Service. But he has big eyebrows and a square chin and hair the color of ink just like Captain Marvel.

In the movie, a woman with a long nose named Barbara Stanwyck gets Fred to murder her husband Edward G. Robinson. What a sucker Fred is.

Billy and me, we've got thirty cents. I have the quarter I got from Mr. George. Billy's got the nickel Mr. George flipped to him for not getting caught and reaching the wall.

We need some more money.

We want to go to the White Tower restaurant and order two orders of French fried potato chips and two cherry Cokes and then go to the Rat Hole theater and get two large popcorns and two medium-sized Orange Crushes.

Here's the money we need:

Two French fries	2 x .10	= .20
Two cherry Cokes	2 x .6	= .12
Two tickets to Rat Hole	2 x .10	= .20
Two popcorns	2 x .5	= .10
Two Orange Crushes	2 x .5	= .10
Total		.72
Money we have from Mr. George:		.30
Money we need:		.42

We go down the alley behind the Français theater and look up to see if the fire-escape door has got the stick in it to hold it open. It has.

I have a plan.

I have my fishing line and lead weight with me that I use for sneaking into the show without paying. I flip the weight up and around the iron ladder and we pull it down. I go around to the front of the theater and walk up and down the lineup. Right away I'm lucky! There's Dick Dork and Dumb Doug.

I tell them that instead of paying thirteen cents to get in to see *Double Indemnity*, I can get them in for ten cents. They give me their dimes and I take them around the back and tell them to wait there with Billy until I find two more.

It doesn't take long.

It's easy to find two kids who want to save three cents each. Six cents can buy you some nice chocolate-covered raisins. I get their dimes.

Around the back I explain to them that they all have to go in together. I tell them they have to crawl in and stay low and roll into the aisle. I tell them about the curtain. How you have to grab the bottom of it.

"If you don't hold the curtain," I say, "it will blow and light will come in and the ushers will come, and you'll get slapped around and then they'll throw you out."

The kids are looking scared. Scared and excited.

Up they go.

When they reach the landing, we let the ladder go and it rises up out of reach.

"Do you think they'll make it?" Billy says.

"If they do as they're told they will," I say.

On the landing, they're crouched together. It looks like they are trying to decide who's going in first. Looks like they've picked Dumb Doug because he's the biggest.

Instead of crawling in like I told him, Dumb Doug grabs the door, opens it wide and walks in. The other three walk in behind him.

Billy and me, we round the corner and hide and peek. Sure enough, very soon an usher sticks his head out the fire-escape door and looks around. Then the door shuts. No stick to hold it open for some fresh air.

Today's going to be extra hot in the Français theater, for sure. And stinking. All the perfume and smelly feet and cigarettes and farts and stale popcorn.

We go around the front and cross the street and watch the ushers come out dragging the four kids by their shirts. Kicked out.

We walk up Dalhoozie and go into the White Tower restaurant. The White Tower is not a tower. It's just a small little square building with a fake castle turret on each corner. The roof is so low Buz Sawyer could probably reach up and put his hand on it.

Inside there are five red stools at the counter.

The French fried potatoes smell delicious, specially with the vinegar and the salt. We can't get cherry Cokes, because we're two cents short. Ordinary Cokes will do.

"I feel sort of bad," says Billy. "That they got caught."

I don't say anything.

"Do you feel bad?" says Billy.

I look right at him. Should I, Granny? Look at this face and believe what I say.

"No, I don't feel bad," I lie. "Serves them right. They didn't do what they were told."

We walk up past the Union Station and the Chateau Laurier. There's a small parade with drums and a trombone and some soldiers who just came home from the war that is almost over.

There are kids riding the iron horses of the War Memorial.

On Sparks Street there's a big fight in front of Bowle's Lunch. There are soldiers rolling on the ground and police and girls screaming. The big window of Bowle's Lunch is crashed in and there's glass all over Sparks Street. There are people still sitting in the restaurant eating mashed potatoes and talking about the fight.

There's a sailor kissing a girl near the shattered window.

Further up Sparks Street I see my father. He's going into the Household Finance Company. He doesn't see me. My mother and father fight all the time about the Household Finance Company.

There's a part of the Ottawa *Journal* on the sidewalk on Bank Street. I pick it up and start to read what's written there. I have to. I can't help it.

Ripley's Believe It Or Not! When it is 90 degrees in the shade where you are there is a place only six miles away that is 60 degrees below zero! Where is it?

"Banana skins fried in cold cream taste something like French fried potatoes!" (says prisoner of war for 3 years)

Will the earth blow up? Atomic war next?

The human body has 206 bones and 696 muscles

Page turner for organist wanted

Soldiers met at Lansdowne Park

The Rat Hole theater on Bank Street is really the Rialto theater but everybody calls it the Rat Hole because they say when you sit there in the dark you can feel the rats jumping around your ankles fighting for the popcorn and candy on the floor down there.

Three Alan Ladd movies today for ten cents!

What a bargain!

Billy and me, we present a little toast to Mr. George with our Orange Crushes. There is no clink when our glasses touch for the toast because our glasses are made of paper.

Not like in the movies.

Alan Ladd is up there on the screen.

Right away the screen goes brown and Alan Ladd disappears and soon we can smell smoke and the lights go on and everybody's yelling and a man comes out on the stage in front of the screen and tells us there'll only be *two* Alan Ladd movies instead of three because one of them just burned up in the projection room and that's that and if anybody wants their money back well, too bad, you're not getting it back and now here's two really good Alan Ladd movies coming up so enjoy yourselves or go to hell home, he doesn't care one way or another...

In the movie *The Glass Key* Alan Ladd wears a long coat with wide shoulders and a hat like my father's hat. He almost never takes off the hat and coat.

He has his hat off once when he's half dead in the hospital bed. And once he has his hat *and* coat off when the bad guy, William Bendix, is throwing him up against the wall like a rubber ball and another time when two other bad guys try to drown him in a tub of ice water.

William Bendix puts a whole onion in a sandwich and stuffs it in his mouth all at once he's such a pig and meanwhile Alan Ladd sets fire to a mattress he's tied to and crashes out a window and down through a glass skylight and escapes. His face is a mess but the next day in the hospital Veronica Lake comes in with her hair falling down over her eye and Alan Ladd is his handsome old self again and you can tell by the music and the way her curly lips are about two stories high on the screen that she wants to kiss him more than anything else in the world.

"SHAZAM!" whispers Billy.

I'm thinking about a girl I remember at York Street School, Geranium Mayburger, who had her very own picture of Alan Ladd in a frame with glass her mother bought her for her birthday at Woolworth's on Rideau. Geranium had the picture on her desk and was kissing it when the teacher, Mr. Blue Cheeks, was telling us the history of the war and he saw her and everything went quiet for a while and then he turned purple and grabbed it from her and smashed it into the wastebasket.

In the other movie, *This Gun for Hire*, Alan Ladd is a nice bad guy who gets up in the morning with all his clothes on, gives his little kitten some milk in a saucer and then shoots a guy and also the guy's secretary who is trying to make him a cup of coffee.

Veronica Lake does magic tricks while she's singing to old drunks sitting at tables. Alan Ladd gets on a train with Veronica Lake who's a spy for the war.

Veronica gets a twisted ankle and her hair falls over her right eye and her mouth gets quite curly. A fat guy who eats peppermints all the time is a traitor and the cops come and gun down Alan Ladd who can't sleep because his cat died.

Veronica Lake says, "You saved my life," and Alan Ladd, even though he's dead, says, "Thanks!" for some reason and that's the end.

We walk up Sparks Street past the Bowle's Lunch smashed window. There's a big board covering the window and all the broken glass is gone. Down the street the Salvation Army is playing some music. Near the War Memorial somebody's making a speech and there's lots of soldiers and girls around.

Up Rideau Street Billy goes into the public library and I go on ahead home. I look in Imbro's Restaurant window at some people eating ice cream sundaes. If I had any money left I'd buy one. Maybe Mr. George tonight at choir will give me another quarter.

He seems to be a nice man.

What he did with the choir cat and his cape.

How he cut the cape so the cat wouldn't have to wake up.

14

A Bad Bing Crosby Habit

EVERYBODY'S EXCITED. Horseball's mother won an electric stove. Worth two hundred dollars! At the Monster Bingo last night. It only cost her fifty cents to play twenty-one games. Fifty cents for a brand new shiny stove!

The stove is on the sidewalk in front of Laflamme's. Everybody's crowded around looking at it, feeling it. It's so shiny and white. It's a Westinghouse — the best kind, somebody says.

Horseball's mother can't stop telling everybody about the bingo. How hot it was there at the Auditorium. How they had big fans blowing air over blocks of ice to cool off the bingo players so they wouldn't sweat so much all over the bingo cards and have the cards always sticking to their arms.

Some of Horseball's sisters pretend they're cooking stuff on the stove.

"I'll cook the supper!" "No, I'll cook the supper!" "No, I will!"

They're shoving each other out of the way.

Now Horseball's father and some of the brothers lift up the stove and take it into the house.

"Careful now!" says Mrs. Laflamme, "Careful you don't scratch the new stove on the door frame. Careful!" Horseball's father and his brothers bang the brand-new stove three times on the doorway on the way in. Everybody's yelling and pushing. They're trying to be the first back in the house after the stove. Some of the small Laflammes climb in the front window. Some are already in the house. They lean out the upstairs windows and shout about the stove and wrestle.

Horseball dumps a pot of water on everybody from the window. There's a big argument about who did it. Everybody's shouting and laughing and running around.

Soon they'll all be back in the house. I could get in line and live with them. Pretend I'm one of the Laflammes.

Back in my house there's torn pages of magazines all over the floor. Phil loves to rip paper. My father says that's how Phil reads. "Tonight," my father often says, "maybe I'll get to read the paper before Phil does!"

My mother's in the kitchen doing the washing. Phil's diapers are going through the wringer. The wringer is like a strange underwater animal with rollers for lips that eat wet cloth. The rollers pull the diapers through, roll the cloth through the tight lips and squeeze out the water.

What it would be like to get your hand caught in there? Pull your arm right in. Wring out your arm.

The diapers fall into a tub and then I take the tub out

the back and hang Phil's diapers on the clothesline to dry
and to be put on him again.

My job.

The torn magazines are *National Geographics*.

That my granny left for me.

At least he didn't tear my two favorite ones — the one
about the beautiful Aztec boy and the one about the trap
door spider that scares me so much I start to shake.

Outside, Mr. Lipshitz is there with his wagon. Some of
the Laflamme boys bring out their old electric stove and
throw it up into his wagon. The wagon sags a bit and the
old horse jumps and says something.

Mr. Lipshitz counts some change out of his little black
purse.

I call on Billy but he's gone ahead.

I cross Angel Square to go to choir this time. So I can
see some of the lacrosse game.

In the winter on Angel Square there are always fights.
But not in the summer. There's no school in the summer.

There's a pretty big crowd at the lacrosse game. There
are two good players that everybody cheers for. One of
them is the smallest on the field. The other one is the
biggest. The small one is a little Pea Soup they call
Sixpouce. Sixpouce means six inches. Whenever Sixpouce
gets the ball in his stick everybody goes wild cheering.
Sixpouce is as quick and tricky as a chipmunk.

The biggest player is a big Dogan they call Goliath.
Whenever Goliath gets the ball in his stick everybody says,
"Oooooo," and, "Oh no, it's Goliath, run for your lives!"

I'm standing beside a family. There's the father and the mother and the two boys — two brothers. The mother's belly is high like my mother's. There's another brother or sister in there waiting to come out and be in the family.

One of the brothers, the older one, is cheering for Sixpouce. The younger brother is cheering for Goliath.

"Come on, Goliath!"

"Come on, Sixpouce!"

Now Sixpouce has the ball in his stick. He runs toward Goliath. Goliath is going to knock him silly and take the ball from him.

Then Sixpouce does something that makes everybody gasp! He ducks and runs right between Goliath's legs and escapes and scores!

The two brothers look at each other. They can't believe it.

The crowd is going wild.

The brothers pretend they are Goliath and Sixpouce.

The younger one crawls between the older one's legs. Their mother and father look at them and laugh. The father laughs and leans and ruffles the boys, hugs the boys. Maybe I could go and live with them.

I often feel like this. Wanting, wondering what it would be like to live in someone else's house.

I leave the game and walk up York Street to King Edward Avenue and up to choir.

I go down the dark stairs to the choir chamber. I hang on to the round wooden railing. It is smooth and larger than my hand. I'm not late so I don't need to skip step number nine.

Just on time.

"Ah!" says Mr. Skippy. "Look, Mr. George, who has arrived to make our ensemble complete! Shall we begin, Mr. George?"

We start choir practice.

Mr. George is playing the piano. Mr. Skippy is listening to us singing. Especially his summer boys. Dick Dork and Dumb Doug won't look at me. They don't know that Billy and I know they got caught by the ushers. They won't say anything about it.

They're too ashamed.

Mr. Skippy is paying attention, listening to me singing. He stops the choir. He's bent over me.

"Rest, Mr. George," he tells Mr. George. "Rest. We have a little tidying up here to do, don't we?"

He's looking at me. Mr. George winks at me. His thick glasses make the wink look like many winks.

"Now," says Mr. Skippy, "do we have a new style of singing here by one of our summer boys? Holding the note longer than is written? O, God our help in *aaaaages* past?"

Mr. George plays it. Making fun. Winking.

"Are we being influenced by some popular trend, Mr. Martin O'Boy?"

"I don't know, sir."

"Well, let's see now, Mr. O'Boy. Who is your favorite singer on the radio?"

"Bing Crosby," I say. "I like 'Moonlight Becomes You.'"

"Aha! Bing Crosby! That's it! That's exactly the way Bing Crosby would sing 'Our help in *aaaaages* past,' dragging the note. Bing Crosby is a crooner, Mr. Martin O'Boy. He's not singing hymns in Mr. Skippy's church choir now, is he? Now that's enough Bing Crosby. No more Bing Crosby. Shall we continue, Mr. George?"

After choir Mr. Skippy says stay for a few minutes with Mr. George to help get rid of this Bing Crosby habit before it's too late. A bad habit. This Bing Crosby.

Mr. George is at the piano. We practice a few verses while everybody's piling out and going home.

Mr. George says my notes are pure. He says my voice is beautiful. I sound as clean as an icicle. As pure as a drop of spring water. Like a beautiful statue of an angel. A drop of quicksilver. A voice from heaven. Like an ice cream sundae.

Everybody's gone now. Except Mr. George and me.

Mr. George gives me a hug in the empty choir room.

He's becoming very fond of me.

"I'm becoming very fond of you, you know that, Martin O'Boy?" says Mr. George.

Mr. Skippy is peeking in the room. Now he comes in. He saw Mr. George give me the hug. He heard him say that he was becoming very fond of me.

"All right, Mr. George," says Mr. Skippy. "That's enough. Time for young summer boys to be going home to their mothers. Remember, Mr. George, we are responsible for these boys. No harm must come to them. We've spoken of this before, haven't we? Now, run along, Martin O'Boy. Goodnight now."

Before I go through the door I look back. They are both watching me go out.

I make step number nine squeak but I wait back on the landing and try to listen.

Mr. Skippy is talking. His voice is serious. It has a warning in it. He sounds like he's scolding Mr. George. It's not an argument though.

Mr. George isn't saying anything.

I go up and out.

15

Buz

PHIL IS asleep.

Lots of Horseball Laflamme's family are snoring through the wall. Mr. Laflamme is coughing.

It's quiet next door at Mrs. Sawyer's. You never hear anything from there. Before Buz went to fly planes in the war there used to be lots of noise from there. Mr. Sawyer always had lots of visitors over and there'd be singing and laughing. And Mr. Sawyer had an accordion and sometimes he'd play it and you'd hear people dancing.

But then he got sick and died in the hospital.

And Buz always had lots of friends coming over to visit him. Buz was friends with everybody. Even us kids. He'd make lemonade sometimes and we'd all play cards and he'd turn up the radio really loud when there was music on like Don Messer's Islanders or Swing and Sway with Sammy Kaye.

And once Buz took Billy and me and some other kids up to Lindsay's record store on Sparks Street and we played records in the little booths there where you could pretend you were going to buy one of the records until they kicked you out.

And once a friend of his from Sandy Hill came over in his convertible car with the top down and Buz got me and Billy and a bunch of other kids and some Laflammes to pile in and we went for a drive all the way out to Britannia and we all went swimming.

And once we got to go with him and his friends to the Auditorium to see the wrestling.

Yvon Robert vs The Mask.

Yvon Robert ripped off The Mask's mask and tried to make him eat it and then The Mask threw Yvon Robert out of the ring and then jumped down and hit him over the head with a chair and the crowd was going wild and Yvon Robert chased The Mask up the aisle where there was a guy selling hot dogs and The Mask knocked down the hot dog guy and stole a big bowl of mustard off his tray and poured mustard all over Yvon Robert's head and then they got back in the ring and Yvon picked up The Mask's mask and choked The Mask with it until he fainted and Yvon Robert was still the champion.

Later that night, after the wrestling, we saw Yvon Robert and The Mask walking together down Argyle Avenue and laughing.

And once, Buz fixed a tough guy from New Edinburgh named Tomato. His real name wasn't Tomato. His real name was Percy Kelso. Buz told us all about him. His nickname was Tomato because his face was so red.

And he had a lisp. Buz told us that when he and Tomato were kids everybody teased Tomato by calling him Perthy Keltho. "Hey, Perthy Keltho, you got a head like a tomato!"

But when he got older he got real tough for some reason and everybody was afraid of him. Afraid of what he would do to them.

Once, Buz told us, Tomato picked a guy he didn't like off Angel Square and stuffed him in somebody's garbage can and rolled him up Clarence Street and then dumped him in Mr. Lipshitz's wagon as he was passing by.

But Buz was friends with Tomato because once he had a big wooden sliver in his hand and it was starting to swell up and Buz pulled it out with a pair of pliers.

Last winter Billy Batson did a very stupid thing. We were going over to Rogers' Drug Store across the St. Patrick Street bridge to New Edinburgh and there was Percy Kelso on the bridge looking down at the ice floating there. On our way by Percy, Billy said really quiet under his breath, "Hello, Mithter Tomato," but Percy heard what Billy said and turned around and reached out as quick as lightning and grabbed Billy and turned him upside down and was holding him by his ankles over the icy Rideau River when along came Buz — lucky for Billy.

Buz talked to Tomato and Tomato put Billy back safe on the bridge and then Buz made Billy and me apologize to *Mister Kelso* — made us say to Tomato (Mr. Kelso) good luck and good health and thank you for allowing us to come over to New Edinburgh and if you ever need any messages delivered or errands run we'd be glad to do it no charge for you, Mister Kelso...

Buz told us after that we were very lucky and that he was pretty sure Tomato would have dropped Billy into the Rideau River and he'd be a Popsicle by now. Right after that Buz went off to war.

Buz took care of us. When he comes home from the war he'll take care of us again. I wish he'd hurry up. We miss Buz.

There's the front door.

My father's home.

It's payday, so he'll be drunk.

I hope he doesn't come in our room and sit on the bed and turn on the light and wake Phil up like he sometimes does. When he does come in he tells me all kinds of stuff about what we're going to do together — go fishing, go to the lumber yard and get some boards and how we're going to build a teeter-totter for Phil and how he's going to buy me things like boxing gloves and roller skates and a bicycle, all that stuff, and the next day he doesn't even remember all the things he said...

Here he comes up the stairs...one step at a time.

Maybe Buz will come home soon and make us all some lemonade...

Now he's in the bathroom. He's so filled up with beer that it takes him forever...

Or Buz's friend will come with the convertible.

Now he sits on their squeaky bed to take off his heavy shoes...

First one shoe hits the floor with a loud bang. Phil makes a grunting noise. Still asleep...

The drunker my father is the more time it takes to drop the other shoe...

I miss my granny. How brave she must have been when she turned around all of a sudden and stabbed that guy near Baron Strathcona's fountain...

It will be a long time before the other shoe falls. I'll get up and take a bath while I'm waiting. Cheap comes with me.

Cheap stands on his hind legs and leans on his elbow on the side of the tub and watches me. Now and then he reaches his right paw down and scoops the water to see how hot it is.

Cheap would like to get in the tub with me. He'd like to sit on my chest and help me wash myself maybe.

I think Cheap wants to be a human, a person, instead of being just a cat. I think he'd like to do the things that I do. I think he'd like to sit at the kitchen table and eat snap crackle and pop with me and maybe when he's half finished, reach over and pull the sugar bowl to him and put some extra sugar in his bowl.

And sometimes when he looks at Phil I think he'd like to tell Phil to quit ruining everything all the time.

And when my father boots the enamel basin, Cheap runs and hides but he peeks out almost right away — even before the basin has stopped rolling — and glares at my father as if to say, "Why are you acting like a common animal?"

I think Cheap would like to come to the show with me. I could buy him a ticket and he could sit in the seat beside me. We could watch Alan Ladd pet his little cat before he goes out and murders people or we could watch Abbott and Costello being scared to death by moving candles and revolving rooms and pictures on the wall with moving eyes that follow them everywhere.

Cheap and I, eating popcorn together at the show.

Maybe we'd get some chocolate-covered peanuts. That would be good. But maybe Cheap wouldn't like the chocolate on the peanuts. He doesn't like chocolate. I remember now. He likes peanuts though. But they stick to his teeth and it takes him about a half an hour to get straightened out after.

And he likes cherry Coke. But I don't think he'd be able to drink with a straw. You need lips to suck on a straw.

Cheap hasn't got lips for some reason.

I go back to bed. Cheap lies next to me.

I'm thinking about Mr. George.

Wondering about him.

BANG! There goes the other shoe.

Tears for my granny now. Sleep now.

16

Ice Cream Sundae

MR. GEORGE says I have to stay after choir again today to work with him to cure the Bing Crosby problem.

"We have to root out this Bing Crosby business, don't we, Mr. O'Boy, before it spreads like wildfire and infects all of our summer boys! Don't you agree?"

Mr. George and I work for a while on staying on the note only as it is written and not dragging it like Bing does. Mr. George tells me I'm improving immensely and then we stop working on the problem and he starts telling me about the war and his adventures there.

Everybody's gone but us.

He tells how he shot a German soldier. How bad he felt after. He still feels bad.

He feels bad because he shot the soldier while he was going to the toilet under a tree in a farmer's field. Squatting there with his pants down. Mr. George feels bad.

96

Are there tears in his eyes behind the thick glasses?

Mr. George tells me that some of his friends are still over in the war but they'll be home soon because the war's almost over. Would I like to meet his friends? He's going to the Union Station one of these days pretty soon to meet them when they arrive. He thinks they'll be coming on a big ship called the *Andrea Doria* to Montreal and then the train to Ottawa. I could go with him to meet them at the Union Station.

We leave the church and walk together down the hill to Rideau Street. He's telling more about the war. How he has seven pieces of steel in his leg. He was wounded in Germany by shrapnel. Shrapnel is little pieces of jagged, dirty metal that fly all over the place like bullets when a shell lands near you and explodes. The pieces of flying metal buzz like bees.

I see Billy coming out of the public library with some books. Billy doesn't see us where we are across the street.

"Let's cross over here," Mr. George says. Then he sees Billy. "Isn't that your friend Billy Batson coming out of the library?"

"Yes, it is," I say. "Billy!" I call out but there's two streetcars going by and Billy doesn't hear me.

"Let's not cross just yet. We don't want to talk to Billy just now, do we?"

The two streetcars are gone and so is Billy.

"He's gone anyway," I say.

"Let's cross then," says Mr. George.

Now we're in front of Imbro's Restaurant.

"Martin O'Boy?" says Mr. George. "I have a splendid idea! Why don't you and I go right into Imbro's here and I shall buy two ice cream sundaes — one for you and one for me. Imbro's is famous for its delicious ice cream sundaes!"

Every time I walk by Imbro's I always look in and see people eating delicious ice cream sundaes but I've never had one.

In Imbro's around the walls there are pictures of ice cream sundaes. The pictures are delicious. They make you want to stand up in the booth on top of the table where you're sitting, stand up and lick the picture of the ice cream dripping over the side of the dish or take a bite out of the picture of the chocolate-covered banana or nibble on the nuts and strawberries covering the Imbro's special butterscotch and caramel sundae.

They have banana splits with chocolate, pineapple or strawberry, hot fudge sundaes with whipped cream. They have butterscotch, Crispy Crunch, mini marshmallows, melon, blueberry, orange, peach, mango, coffee...

Some of the sundaes in the pictures are in long curved dishes that are flat. Some are in tall vases narrow at the bottom and wide at the top. You get a spoon with a long handle if you pick a tall one.

"I think I want the double banana split with chocolate *and* pineapple," says Mr. George.

I can't make up my mind. Mr. George is sitting on the same side of the booth as I am. I'm pushed up close to the wall so it's hard to look up to see all the pictures up there. He's pressed against me.

There's one I see that is different than all the others. It's called a David Harum. I don't know what that is, a David Harum. But the picture looks good. The ice cream is not dribbling over the side and the dish is a different kind, not tall, not long and flat.

"Why don't you try the David Harum?" Mr. George says.

"David Harum," I say.

"Good choice," says Mr. George.

Now right away I want to change my mind but it's too late. The lady is writing down what we want on her little pad.

She sticks her pencil behind her ear in her hair.

"Another young choir singer, Mr. George?" she says.

"Yes, he's a beautiful singer," Mr. George tells her.

"Aren't they all," she says. "Aren't they all!"

Then she says, "Interesting shoes you've got, son. Waiting to grow into them, are ya?" Then she laughs.

Mr. George says he's been meaning to ask me about the shoes, about how long they are.

I tell him about the shoes and the drunk man at Lefebvre's Shoe Market. Mr. George looks really interested in my story about the shoes. He shakes his head and smiles. He likes me very much. His face shows it.

The lady with the pencil in her hair is back. She puts the sundaes down. Mr. George's banana split is half the size of the table. It has four scoops of ice cream drowned in chocolate and pineapple and sprinkled with nuts and a red cherry on each scoop and two bananas, split long ways, surrounding the ice cream.

Mr. George digs in.

My granny always said that when she slammed down the porridge bowl in front of me: "Dig in!"

My sundae is different than Mr. George's. It's a lot smaller — about the size of a saucer. It's only one scoop. And no dribbling over the side. And there's not much sauce in it. And there's no cherry. And there's one nut cut in half sitting on the top.

And there's greenish brown liquid under the scoop of ice cream.

"You got the most expensive one," says Mr. George. "It must be really good!"

I take my first taste with the short small spoon. I've never tasted anything like this. It's a bit like peppermint but not really. And there's a bit of a burning feeling but the ice cream makes it go away. And there's a sniff or a taste, a little bit sour, like I sniff sometimes from my father in the bathroom — the Aqua Velva.

I bite the nut in half and mix it with the ice cream and the greenish brown sauce. The taste goes up my nose and makes my eyes water.

Mr. George is digging in. He looks like some of the men in Bowle's Lunch shoveling in a whole pile of meat and potatoes. I'm eating bites so small I must look like a chipmunk nibbling away on sunflower seeds.

We're done. Mr. George gives money at the pay counter to the lady with the pencil stuck through her head.

"How're ya feelin', sonny? Hope you don't have too big of a hangover tomorrow." Then she laughs. "There's crème de menthe and brandy in that little David Harum. Just a couple tablespoons each. Never hurtcha! HA! HA!"

Her mouth is opening huge and I can see right down her throat because she's leaning over the counter and down to me.

The pencil looks as big as a log.

"Straight home!" she roars and Mr. George takes me by the hand.

17

Heney Park

IT'S NOT far to Heney Park. The park looks beautiful ahead in the moonlight. The shape of the trees and then the hill in the middle and the gazebo on the top with the six stone legs and the pretty pointed roof.

We always go up there in the winter, us kids, when it's icy, with our sleighs made of cardboard boxes, and slide. I'm imagining it's winter and the trees are coated with clear crystal ice. But it's not winter and it's not ice, it's moonlight.

Mr. George is telling me about the war and the woman he saved from drowning in France. He carried her to her house and brought her back to life and she cooked him up a big meal of truffles which are like mushrooms only better.

And then they made a fire in her fireplace.

When we were in Imbro's waiting for our ice cream sundaes Mr. George showed me his war medals. Both medals had six points like a star. They had King George's crown on and in a circle in the middle of the star, the words, "The France and Germany Star" and on the other one, "The Italy Star." One had a ribbon with blue and white and red stripes. The other one had white and red and green stripes.

After they lit the fire, she took all her clothes off, I think, and hung them up to dry by the fire. Mr. George says let's go up the hill to the gazebo, see what the moonlight looks like from up there.

There's no bench there. I want to sit down. Mr. George wants me to stay standing up. He's fiddling with his pants. I can see him in the dark.

In the war, while the clothes were drying, Mr. George said the woman he saved had lots of nice hair between her legs.

"Do you have any hair between your legs?" says Mr. George.

"I'm dizzy," I say. "I want to sit down."

He says I'm such a good singer in the choir. The best singer in the choir. He wants to give me a hug because I'm such a good singer. I can't see his face.

Then he doesn't give me a hug. He pulls me behind one of the stone pillars of the gazebo.

"Shh!" he says. "There's somebody coming. Some boys. We don't want them to hear us. I don't like those boys."

We hide behind the pillar. The moon is shining along the side of the hill. The boys are wrestling up and down the hill and laughing. In the moonlight each boy has a shadow wrestling the shadow of another boy. They wrestle and push down the hill and into the dark under the big trees. It's quiet again.

"Let's go down under the big trees and sit on one of the benches down there. It's a beautiful moonlit night and you don't have to go home just yet," says Mr. George.

We go down the hill and he takes my hand. His hand is big. Bigger than my father's. Bigger than Ketchy Balls'.

"You are a beautiful boy," he says. "Maybe you'll sing for me."

We sit on the bench under the big trees. The moonlight is on the hill and over the leaves of the big trees above us. The boards of the bench feel rough on my legs. If I move back it's better. When I move back I have to push my toes into the small stones on the walk in front of us. Some of the moon shows between the leaves of the big trees above us and shines on the small stones like jewels.

"If you sing for me," says Mr. George, "I'll give you one of my war medals. Sing that Bing Crosby song…"

"Moonlight becomes you," I sing softly. "It goes with your hair…You certainly know the right things to wear…"

He puts his left arm around my back and his hand into the left pocket of my shorts and pushes his fingers between my legs.

"How's yours?" he's whispering. "How's yours?" He takes my right hand in his hand and puts it in his lap. There's something there like the railing going down the dark back stairs to the choir room.

"Keep going, O'Boy! Oh, boy, keep going!"

He's whispering loud and rough.

The moon stares through the leaves at us.

He pulls me tight against him with his left arm so I can hardly breathe.

"I can't breathe," I try to yell. There's wet on my wrist and on my arm.

Now there's a crunching sound along the path.

Footsteps in the dark coming. Crunching.

Mr. George gets up off the bench so fast he knocks me onto the path. He disappears behind the big tree behind our bench. Two people come along the walk. I get back on the bench. The boy and the girl stop under the park light up the path. They kiss each other. Now they walk closer. My knee is cut from the stones. They stop right in front of my bench and he kisses her. They don't even notice me. I don't breathe. They start walking again. I get off the bench and walk after them. I catch up to them but on the grass — no crunching. I try to keep my shoes from flap slapping.

When I'm far enough away from Mr. George's hiding tree I duck into the bushes and trip on my shoes and roll into some cobwobbly sticky stuff. I'm rolling in it and the dirt and dead leaves and twigs and bugs and spider webs. It's all between my fingers and around my arms and in my hair and around my legs and in my face. I'm in a huge spider's web and rolling around under the bushes.

Now it's Mr. George whispering as loud as he can.

"Boyo! Boy O'Boy! Where are you? Come out! Don't be afraid! I won't hurt you! Boyo! I love you!"

I can't get my breath. Sticky strings of web are covering my mouth and nose. I'm afraid I'm going to scream.

There's an opening in the hedge I'm under. I roll through it down a steep bank onto the sidewalk and over the curb into a muddy puddle in the gutter. The puddle is slimy and greasy and I can smell car oil and dog turds.

I see Mr. George thrash his way out of the hedge in the dark between two streetlights. I lie still in the gutter and sidespy up at him. He's looking up and down Heney Street, calling now, "Boyo! Boy O'Boy! Don't hide on me!"

He seems afraid, the way he's looking back and forward. Back and forward. This way. That way.

"Boyo!"

He pushes back into the hedge. Maybe I'm still in there.

Here come the lovers again. They're on the sidewalk right where I'm lying. They're having another hug. Haven't they had enough hugs? What's the matter with them, anyway? Now they're kissing again.

I come out of my puddle on my hands and knees. Now I stand up. I'm like something out of a horror comic coming out of a slimy lagoon. A creature. The girl screams. The boy jumps back. He takes her hand and pulls her down the street.

I run down Heney Street to Cobourg.

I stop to get my breath in front of Lachaine's store. Mrs. Sawyer comes out. She has a bag in her arm with a loaf of bread sticking out.

"Good evening, Martin," she says, surprise in her voice and comes over to me. I'm looking in Lachaine's window at the stuff in there. Potatoes and hard candy and bars of soap and caps for cap guns and yo-yos and black and red licorice and shoelaces and bobby pins for your hair and a box of red beets. And Lachaine's black store cat asleep curled in the corner.

And I am also looking at myself in the glass.

"How are you this evening, Martin O'Boy?" says Mrs. Sawyer.

I look up at her.

"Why are you crying?" says Mrs. Sawyer.

"I'm not crying," I say. "I don't think."

"You seem to be crying," she says.

"There's something in my eye maybe," I say.

"Is there something in both your eyes?"

"I guess so."

"You have to be very careful of your eyes," says Mrs. Sawyer. "They're the only eyes you have." She goes back a step and looks me up and down. "And your knee is bleeding. Bleeding bad. You'd better be going on home now. It's getting late, don't you think? What have you been doing? Look at you!"

"I'm... I was fighting after choir. Just playing. Wrestling in the park. After choir. Play fighting. Like we used to do with Buz..."

"You'd better come home. I'll walk with you. Your mother's going to be worried..."

"I'm going in the store...and then I'm going right home..."

"Your mother's going to be worried...you look like you

107

just lost your best friend..." She turns and moves away. "Straight home now," she calls back.

I pretend to go into the store but I don't.

After a while I go down Cobourg and to my house at 3 Papineau. I stand at the door. I don't want to cry. I'll show my mother my knee but I won't cry. I'll tell her about fighting after choir. She'll see my knee and take care of it.

I open the door. The door to the house where I don't want to live.

Please, somebody. Take care of me. Love me.

18

The Riddle and a Letter

WE'RE EATING bacon for breakfast this morning. My father's late for work so he's eating the bacon standing up. The bacon is a bit burnt. My mother and father just had a big fight about it. My mother's gone back upstairs with Phil. Phil howled all the way up. He always howls when my parents fight.

He's howling now. Lenny Lipshitz can probably hear him all the way down at number nine.

"You know," my father says, "your mother once went to the doctor to have her head examined but they couldn't find anything."

It's an old joke. I've heard it many times.

I give Cheap a piece of bacon under the table.

"Don't feed that cat bacon. It's expensive," my father says.

I look in my father's face. I don't say what I'm thinking.

"He doesn't care about you, you know," my father says. "He only cares about food."

"Cheap likes me, I can tell," I say.

"Animals aren't like people. Cats don't act like people. People like you or they don't like you. Cats just care about food."

"I think Cheap loves me," I say. "The way he looks at me. With his ripped-out ear like that."

"Are you the one who feeds him?" my father says.

"When I eat, he eats. I feed him off my plate. Nobody else feeds him but me. He's my cat. He gets what I get."

Cheap's looking out from under the table up at my father. Cheap doesn't like my father. You can tell the way he puts his good ear down. And his eyes wide open. He's waiting to see if my father's going to kick something. His legs are ready to get himself out of the way. A flying basin goes bouncing one way, Cheap will head the other way.

And when Old Faithful gushes, Cheap is already gone.

"He only cares about you because you're the one who feeds him," my father says, putting on his hat to go to work.

No, that's not true. He loves me. I can tell when I talk to him and he closes his eyes. Squeezes them shut. Like he's having a good time.

"Cheap is a joke for a cat. As far as I'm concerned, this cat is just a waste of fur. And don't feed him bacon. Bacon is expensive!"

My father slams out the door.

He didn't even notice my slashed knee.

Cheap is staring up at me.

I pick him up and he gives me a little purr.

"You're not a joke," I say to him and give him some more bacon.

"And you're not a waste of fur. Maybe somebody we know is a waste of skin! What do you think of that?"

Cheap agrees.

I'm sitting on our front step with my wool sweater pulled around me. Cheap sits with me.

Cheap saw what happened last night.

Last night Phil got his arm caught in the wringer.

Soon as I got in the house to show my mother my slashed knee I heard Phil starting to howl. I ran in the kitchen and bumped into my mother's belly. Phil's hand was coming out of the other side of the wringer. The lips eating Phil. My mother started pounding the safety bar. The safety bar on top of the wringer to release Phil. Phil being gobbled up.

Hit the safety bar hard! We were hitting it, my mother and me.

"Hit it! Hit it!" my mother was screaming. Phil was making choking noises and biting his tongue, chewing on his tongue. Phil's arm was halfway through when the wringer snapped open and Phil fell back and his arm slid out like a piece of raw meat.

Then we held Phil while my mother ran cold water over his arm and bathed it gently with soap and rinsed the flesh some more. Phil was staring straight ahead. No sounds.

"He's in shock," she said. "We have to wrap him up warm. We'll get the doctor tomorrow."

We wrapped Phil's arm in clean cloths and I made him some warm cocoa and we put him gentle into his iron bed and my mother lay down with him and held him and he sobbed some and my mother sang him a song:

> *Old Mother Hubbard*
> *Went to the cupboard*
> *To give her poor dog a bone*
> *When she got there*
> *The cupboard was bare*
> *And so her poor dog had none.*

After Phil was asleep, she whispered to me, "I don't know what I'd do without you." Then she noticed my knee. "You've cut your knee," she said. "Put some iodine on it and I'll look at it tomorrow...and maybe you should have a bath. You're filthy. What have you been doing anyway? I thought you were at choir. I hope you haven't been misbehaving...remember...the one we're counting on..."

Soon she was asleep too. Mother and Phil cuddled up.

I had a bath, put on the iodine, went to bed and had this awful dream. A boy (me) is swimming in the Rideau River at Dutchie's Hole, near where my granny used to live. Another boy (Phil) is standing on the shore. The water around the boy is full of floating pigs' heads and guts and turds from the slaughterhouse. The boy spits in the water. The boy on the shore yells, "Stop spitting in the water, you're spoiling everything for the other swimmers!" My granny, who is standing on an iron train bridge, is calling out to the boy not to listen to this foolishness. The boy in the water yells, "Phil, you're ruining everything, not me!"

On the steps this morning I'm reading things from the Ottawa *Journal* to Cheap while I'm hugging my knees. The enamel basin is on the sidewalk in front of Lenny Lipshitz's place three doors down. I'll get it after.

I read to Cheap that so far, 45 million people got killed in the war that is just about over. I wonder where they put all the bodies. How many big black cars came.

Eh, Granny?

I read to Cheap about my father's razor blades. Blue Gillette Blades — the sharpest, smoothest finished edges ever honed. That must be why my father cuts himself all the time. Little pieces of white toilet paper stuck to his face with a spot of red.

I read to Cheap about the Carnation Milk Baby. His picture is on every can of Carnation Milk. The most beautiful baby in the Dominion of Canada.

My granny said I could have been that baby but there was no picture of me to send.

I read about the atomic bomb. A new bomb that is very small but could blow up a whole city and everybody in it. Kill everybody.

Will the whole world blow up eventually, the paper says. They can drop the bomb from 6 miles up in the air where it's always very cold.

That's it! The answer to the riddle in Ripley's Believe or Not!

I read my horoscope to Cheap who is asleep beside me.

My father calls it horrorscope. "*LEO. You will, in the next few days, come into a large bounty.*" Bounty means money or riches. I read that in the *National Geographic* about the Aztecs. Next I'm reading about a crazy millionaire who comes to Ottawa sometimes from Merrickville and goes to the Union Station when the soldiers come home from the war on the train and gives out fifty-dollar bills to the heroes coming home...

Oh, no! Here come the ketchup lady and the turkey lady.

"There you are! Good morning, Martin. How are you?" says the turkey lady.

I don't answer but I say this, "I'm thinking of a riddle. Where is it so hot where you are that you could fry an egg on the sidewalk but there is a place only six miles away that is 60 degrees below zero. Where is it?"

"Mmm," says the turkey lady, "how fascinating. Let me see..." The ketchup lady is looking at my shoes. My shoes are filthy from last night. They don't look new anymore.

"You got the shoes," says the ketchup lady. "Good. Where did the shoes come from? Are they someone else's shoes?"

"No, they're not someone else's shoes, they're my shoes."

"But they're not new shoes..."

"Yes, they are. New shoes. My new shoes." I'm giving her my honest face as hard as I can. The face that people will always want to believe.

"Did you see that enamel basin down the street there? In front of number nine? My father kicked that basin all the way down there. Our basin."

"Oh, my…"

"And the riddle?" says the turkey lady. "Is it a trick question?"

"No trick," I say. "Just look up."

They both look up.

While they're both looking up, my door opens and my mother comes out. Then the three go in the house to talk about me. And maybe the enamel basin…

I feel invisible.

Along comes Billy. He starts telling me about Mr. George. How Mr. George told him he is going to play a special piece on the organ at a church service one Sunday morning. Not a choir piece. But a special piece — just Mr. George. I don't tell Billy about what happened last night. I don't tell Billy how I hate Mr. George.

The mailman goes by.

Nothing for us. He looks at my shoes.

"Quite the shoes," he says.

He puts a letter through Mrs. Sawyer's door.

He moves on.

A streetcar goes by with nobody on it but the driver. How many dead people you could put in there and take away…the streetcar's red though…you'd have to paint it black…

Mrs. Sawyer's door opens. She's got a letter in her

hand. She's waving it. She looks up and down Papineau Street. Nobody but us. She comes rushing over. She's crying.

"Buz," she says. "My son! He's coming home…any day now!"

19
"Happy Birthday!"

TODAY'S MY birthday. Billy's coming with me for ice.
It's hot again. We're talking about what was in the letter Mrs. Sawyer got from Buz. Buz's real name is Sydney
Sawyer. In the air force he's Flight Lieutenant Sydney
Sawyer. In the letter he said he was wounded. His plane hit
another plane on the aircraft carrier. But not too hard. He
broke a bone in his wrist. He's coming home on the ship
the *Andrea Doria*.

"There are 696 muscles and 206 bones in Buz's body.
And he only broke one of those bones," I say.

"I'll be glad when he comes home. I hope it's soon,"
says Billy. Then he's quiet. Billy's always quiet now.
Looking far away. He's not the same as he was. After that
night when his father escaped from the loony bin. I feel
like asking Billy when's your father coming back from the
war but I won't. Too mean.

I tell him instead about my horrorscope. About the
bounty. Billy tells me about a dream he always has of

finding money — pennies and nickels on the ground and then seeing more and more quarters and fifty-cent pieces and bigger silver dollars and he's picking as many of them up as he can but he can't hold any more and they're spilling all over the place and people are coming to take it all away.

At the ice house it's the same man who gave me the small block the last time.

"Hi, there, pretty boy! Didn't grow into those shoes yet, eh? And who's your little friend? What's your name, little friend?"

"His name's Billy," I say.

"I'm not askin' you. Am I askin' you? I'm askin' him. What's your other name, Billy?"

"Batson. Billy Batson."

"Oh! Like in the comics. Captain Marvel. SHAZAM! Let's see you say SHAZAM! See what happens."

"He doesn't want to," I say.

"Who's askin' you? Shut up, pretty boy. Go ahead. Say it. SHAZAM! Let's see what happens. I'll give pretty boy a nice big block of ice today if you do."

Billy waits a bit and then says a little shazam that you can hardly hear.

"I don't hear no big BOOM! Do you? Wait a minute. Aren't you Art Batson's boy? Guy who lost his mind? Went nuts. Started attacking people? Sure you are. You were just a little kid then. Before the war. They put him away. I worked at the slaughterhouse with him — somewhere like that. Or was it at the paper mill? I forget. That's you, all right. Yeah. His brain just went nuts. Started assaulting strangers. They locked him up…"

We can hear the little bell from the Good Shepherd Convent down the street. Pretty little bell. They ring it at noon always.

Billy's sobbing.

"It's not him," says Billy. Billy's looking down.

Pisspot-head stares for a long time at Billy. Then he looks at me, says this to me…

"Well, maybe I'm wrong. There's lots of crazy people around. Maybe I've got the wrong guy." He gives me a wink. "Here's an extra big block of the best hard ice for your wagon. And here's a sack to cover it. If you hurry home, maybe none of it will be melted! Okay, Billy Batson?"

I don't say anything. I want this big block of ice. It's my birthday, you know.

Outside Petigorsky's Shoe Repair on St. Patrick Street old man Petigorsky is out sweeping off his front step. I can tell he can hear my shoes flopping on the sidewalk. He stops sweeping and watches my shoes coming.

"Boys, boys," he says smiling, "I know you can't stop because of the ice you have maybe melting but you know I could shorten those shoes for you in a jiffy no charge."

"You could shorten the shoes?"

"Easy," he says. "I would just whack the front ends off them mit my little machete! Like a circumcision! HA! HA! HA! You wouldn't even have to take them off! HA! HA! HA!"

Really funny, Mr. Petigorsky.

At home Billy helps me with the block of ice. We use the ice tongs and we both carry the big block into the kitchen. We get on two chairs and lift the heavy ice up and into the top of the ice box.

My mother is out in the yard with Phil. I can see on the table flour and a bowl and some baking powder and vanilla and squares of chocolate.

Looks like we might be having a birthday cake.

I've got two cents in my pocket so I ask Billy if he wants to go over to Prevost's store on Cobourg and get a grab bag and watch the hundred-year-old fly swatter.

When the time is right I'm going to ask Billy to say the truth about his father.

In the store we get the grab bag and open it and share. Billy likes the blackballs and I don't so the sharing is easy. I like the gum drops, he doesn't.

The old man is in his chair in the corner. He's the fly swatter. He is Mr. Prevost's grandfather. The chair they've got him in is like a kid's highchair with a tray in front. On the tray there's spilt sugar. The old man has a fly swatter in each hand sticking straight up from each bony fist. He doesn't move. He doesn't blink. He doesn't even seem to be breathing. He's waiting for nineteen flies to be there at once. Mr. Prevost told me that his record is eighteen. That was last Christmas. But they were tame flies that they bought the old man for Christmas from Radmore's pet shop. Dr. Radmore used to grow flies in an incubator to sell to people with pet snakes and frogs before they put him in jail for torturing dogs and cats.

But it's going to be very hard for the old fly swatter to break the record because these are wild and wild flies are a lot smarter and quicker.

The old man waits.

There are twelve there. But they keep coming and going. Off to the side where the old man's eyes are looking now there are two more flies, one on top of the other, buzzing very loud. The old man's eyes are glistening. He doesn't want to break the record. He wants these two.

Down come the two swatters. One on the buzzing two. The other on the group of twelve.

Direct hit!

The old man's toothless mouth gapes open and he laughs like a goat.

"THEY NEVER KNEW WHAT HIT 'EM!" he shouts. "They never knew what hit 'em!"

"Billy," I say. "Look at me."

Billy looks up from the dead flies into my face. I give him the face that my granny said everybody would have to believe.

"Will you tell me the truth, Billy, if I ask you?"

Billy's lips are black from the blackballs.

"SHAZAM!" says Billy.

"Was that your father that night, when the police came? Was it, Billy?"

"BOOM!" says Billy.

"Was it, Billy?"

"Yes," says Billy.

We go home to my place to see if there's anything going on about my birthday.

My mother asked some people to come over and have a piece of birthday cake. Lenny Lipshitz and his mother came over and had a piece but they left right away. Lenny said he had to go because he was supposed to help his father put a new shoe on their old horse, but the way Lenny looked when he told about the horse made everybody believe it was a lie.

My mother just had time to explain to Mrs. Lipshitz about the writing on the cake before they left.

The cake said:

HAPPY BIRTHDAY
PHIL
A

You see, while she was writing on the cake with the squeeze thing she had to stop and put it down because there was a pot boiling on the stove. Soon as her back was turned Phil grabbed the squeeze thing and fell down the cellar stairs with it and broke it so she couldn't finish writing

— ND
MARTIN

Billy wants the piece of cake with the A on it. A for ATLAS for STAMINA.

Mrs. Batson stayed home, too sad to come. Mrs. Sawyer

sits on the good side of the couch with her saucer of cake and reads the letter from Buz for the hundredth time.

The boat Buz is coming home on is named the *Andrea Doria*. Any day now. Any day.

Horseball and some Laflammes come over and finish the cake. Horseball's trying to get everybody to sing the birthday song but soon as it gets started in comes Mr. Laflamme trying to tell everybody something but he's coughing so much we can't understand him but he at last gets it out.

"...on the radio...atomic bomb...Japan..."

We all pile out the door and into the Laflammes' house to listen to their radio. (We can't hear anything on our radio because the tubes are too weak.)

Laflammes' radio tells us that a whole city in Japan was wiped out and thousands of people were killed by one bomb. An atomic bomb.

The name of the bomb was Little Boy.

And now the war will be over for sure.

Cheap and I, we're imagining what it would be like if they dropped the atomic bomb, Little Boy, on Papineau Street at the corner of Cobourg. Everything flattened. All as flat as Angel Square. Everybody dead. Dead as Granny. Burnt up. My mother and the baby inside her and my father and Grampa in the Home and all the Laflammes and Billy and his mother and his one-eyed father wherever he is and Mrs. Sawyer and Lenny Lipshitz and his mother and his father and his father's horse and the human fly swatter and...

Just Cheap and me standing there alone for some reason. A miracle.

And then through the smoke comes Buz. Out of the cloud of dust walks Buz with his kit bag over his shoulder…and we run up to him…trying to explain…

I guess they never knew what hit 'em!

"Well," I say to Cheap. "Happy birthday, Martin O'Boy!"

And now I just thought of something.

Cheap and me, we didn't get any cake.

20

Mr. George Borrows a Boy

Mr. George is not at choir practice tonight. He's in the church, though. He's above us practicing a fancy piece on the pipe organ for Reverend's special Service of Celebration when the war gets over, which will be pretty soon now because everybody in Japan is practically dead from the atomic bomb, Little Boy.

Down through the heat pipes we can hear the music pounding. We can hardly sing our hymns everything is so loud. And Mr. Skippy's foot is slapping, slapping to keep our beat, so we can practice even though Mr. George is trying to drown us out. The music he's playing is called CROWN IMPERIAL. A celebration! He plays so loud, he plays so happy, so joyous. I can just see his face, his many eyes flashing, he's in heaven. Oh Boy. Oh Boy. Oh Boy.

Around the middle of our practice, while Mr. Skippy is flapping his loose foot on the floor keeping time, we hear the organ stop and soon we hear stair number nine creak and Mr. George comes in. He doesn't even look at me and I don't look at him.

"Mr. Skippy, may I borrow one of your summer boys to come up to the chapel with me and turn the pages of my music for me while I'm practicing?"

Mr. George is looking over the choir. His eyes are sweeping over the group, the thick glasses glittering from the ceiling lights, his eyes looking like many eyes. He's going to pick one of us. I'm sure it's going to be me, his favorite. If it's me I'm not going. I'm going to say I have to leave early to mind my brother — it's an emergency.

"Of course," says Mr. Skippy, "you may borrow one of the boys. Take your pick. Choose one, any one!"

Mr. George's eyes go right over me and onto Billy.

"Billy, you'll come and help me out, won't you, like a good lad...come along."

Billy and Mr. George leave together.

Mr. George has his big hand on Billy's shoulder.

I hate Mr. George.

I'd like to fix him some way. Hurt him. But I don't know what to do. What would my granny do? Turn around real quick and stab him in the face!

Choir practice is over.

Little Boy killed 150,000 people, the paper said.

That's a lot of black cars, Granny.

Somebody fixed the light in the stairs so it's not dark there anymore. You don't have to hang on to the railing to go up and down. Mr. George is still practicing. The pipe organ is shaking the walls. You can feel the rumbling in the wooden stairs.

Out on King Edward Avenue you can hear Mr. George's special music. It's rumbling behind the stained-glass windows of the church. Low notes rumbling and high notes running up and down like pretty water.

I walk a little further down the hill. Music far away now. I wonder what it sounds like up in the organ loft where Mr. George put us that day, right inside the music — all those organ pipes. Me and the summer boys.

Down near the corner of King Edward and Rideau there's another street dance party. There are sailors dancing with pretty girls. The girls are wearing the sailors' hats tilted on their heads. A Glen Miller record is playing over the loud speakers. There are soldiers there too. The sailors are saying that they can dance better than the soldiers.

The soldiers say yeah, maybe, but they can kiss more girls than the sailors can and everybody laughs.

I can't hear Mr. George's music at all from here. The church is up the hill and far away.

What could I do to hurt Mr. George?

What could I do, Granny?

21

That's What You Get

IT'S OVER! The war's over! There's another atomic bomb!
"City wiped off Jap map!" says the Ottawa *Journal*.
The city is called Nagasaki. The name of the bomb this
time is Fat Man.

Thousands and thousands of people are burnt alive.
More black cars, Granny.

Everybody's going wild. They gave up! It's over! They
couldn't take it anymore. Two atomic bombs. Wiped out,
flattened two cities in Japan!

There are parties everywhere. They're getting ready for
a big party on Cobourg Street. The streets are full of torn
paper and bottles and confetti and glass from last night
when everybody ran out of their houses and got drunk.

Everybody wants to have a parade. Be in a parade.
Bring something to make noise with! Near the corner of
St. Patrick and Cobourg there's a flat wagon. Some people
are building a gallows, where you hang people until they
are dead. They're painting a sign. So far it says HANG H.

My mother's belly is so big she can hardly walk. The baby was supposed to come a few days ago. Around the time everybody got killed in Japan. Now everybody's killed again but the baby still won't come out. Scared maybe.

Near Petigorsky's Shoe Repair a bunch of people are making a huge body out of straw and old clothes. There's a sign beside the straw body that says HIROHITO.

"What's a Hirohito?" some kid says.

"Hirohito is the king of Japan," I say. I guess the kid never reads the paper.

The Lee Kung Laundry is closed. No steam pouring out the door. But there's music and singing pouring out the upstairs windows.

I walk up York Street to the Lafayette beer parlor. There's a big fan vent flapping away in the wall beside the door blowing cigarette smoke and beer fumes and stomach gas out onto the street. There's a roar of talking and shouting behind the door. I push open the door and stick my head in to see if I can see my father. The fumes and belches and smoke and noise hit me in the face like a slab of wood. I can't see if he's in there or not. The place is full of men and smoke and shouting and singing and laughing and bottles and glasses clinking and rattling and breaking and pounding on tables. The men at the table near the door look at my head peeking in.

"Get out!" they all say. "Come back in ten years!" And then they all laugh. Now I see my father further in but he doesn't see me. He's telling a joke and everybody's laughing. My father's very funny when he's out.

He's not always funny when he's at home.

I could never tell my father what Mr. George made me do. What he did in Heney Park. My father wouldn't help me, I know he wouldn't. He'd probably say, "…that's what you get for spending your time singing with the Protestants…"

On the doors of Woolworth's on Rideau there are some printed signs stuck there. One sign says:

> *FOR SALE.*
> *Army uniforms. War medals.*
> *(ask inside)*

Why would anybody want to sell their army uniform? Sell their medals? The other signs say:

> *GIRL TO IRON, WASH DISHES.*
> *Twice weekly Evenings 30 cents per hour*

> *BED SITTING ROOM.*
> *1 quiet girl — $30.00 a month — Catherine Street.*

> *DURATION LEG-DO.*
> *Sheer looking as nylons! Big 4 ounce bottle only 49 cents!*
> *Creamy Golden Velvety Skin tone*

I have to read everything. I can't help it.

I'm imagining the Quiet Girl in the Bed Sitting Room spreading the Creamy Golden Velvety Skin guck on her legs to look like nylon stockings before she goes out to get the job Twice Weekly Evenings ironing and washing the dishes. I know you wash dishes but I didn't know you ironed dishes.

There's a big party starting on Confusion Square. The war monument is crawling with kids riding the huge black iron horses and sitting on the iron soldiers' shoulders and helmet heads and riding the big black gun. They're hiding under the wheels of the big gun. They're under the wheels and under the horses' iron feet. If the horses move and the gun rolls, they will be crushed. But it can't happen, Granny, it's only a statue.

And I can't tell my mother about Mr. George because she wouldn't know what to do and just cry and burn the pots on the stove and Phil would start howling and bawling.

Slab wood trucks and coal trucks are driving around full of people with signs and flags. *It's over* say the signs. And *Hang Hirohito!*

A milkman's horse still has his feedbag tied on his head. He's nodding to get the oats up into his mouth. There's a Union Jack flag stuck down into the bag. When the horse nods, the flag waves.

And I can't tell Mr. Skippy. Because maybe he wouldn't believe me and anyway he's Mr. George's friend.

I go down toward the Français theater.

People are yelling at people on their verandas and hanging out windows.

"Soon there'll be no more gas rationing!"

"So what? You haven't got a car anyway!"

Playing at the Français theater is *Buck Privates* starring Abbott and Costello. Bud and Lou go in the army by mistake. The Andrews Sisters sing "Boogie Woogie Bugle Boy." I saw it.

I go down the alleyway behind the theater to see if the fire-escape door is open. There's a small lineup for the movie. Maybe I can make some money.

The fire escape door's not open. No money to be made today.

Around the front, going into the show, I see Mr. George. And going in with him...

Is Billy Batson!

22

Granny's Umbrella

FLAP SLAP, slap flap. I'm heading home.

The streets are full. People are kissing and dancing. Bobby soxers and old men. Flags are waving. Car horns. Noise makers. Confetti. Snakes of people. Kids cheering, dogs barking, babies and old people being pushed in carriages and chairs, boys running and darting in and out, girls laughing and flirting and fixing each other's ribbons.

Here comes Mr. Lipshitz in his wagon. He looks awake. His wagon is full of kids banging pans and pots with sticks. His horse looks like he's walking straighter than he usually does. He's celebrating too.

It starts pouring hot rain.

"It's only a shower! Just a shower! Keep dancing! Let's get soaking wet!"

There's blocked traffic. Dynamite caps exploding under the wheels of the streetcars. Decorated cars and ice trucks and milk wagons, beer in the gutter, church bells ring, firecrackers, rockets, whistles, bonfires, little parades, sticks and pots, banging, rubbing washboards, blowing old bugles, burning and hanging Hirohito, stringing paper on the wires, soaked to the skin, sirens, streetcar bells, school bells, train whistles...

In the middle of the lacrosse field on Angel Square there's a piano sitting. A guy is playing "Roll Out the Barrel!" and a little crowd is singing it.

All of a sudden an awful thought covers me like a big black blanket.

Mr. George is going to do the same thing to Billy as he did to me.

There's a stack of horseballs steaming in rainwater. The horseballs remind me of Buz Sawyer playing hockey. Buz, the best stick handler on the street.

In the winter we use a frozen horseball as a puck. The street is our rink. We use the snowbanks as the boards for the rink. The rink is five blocks long. Cobourg Street from Rideau down to St. Patrick. Everybody on the street plays. Buz can stickhandle a frozen horseball through everybody all the way down the street. There's usually two teams. Buz is on one team. Everybody else is on the other team. He starts at the top of the street and stickhandles the frozen horseball for five blocks through every kid in Lowertown who wants to try and stop him.

He's also the best shooter.

He can wrist shot the frozen horseball and knock the mailman's hat off. He can drive one through your mail slot. He's the best. I wish he was here right now. He'd tell me what to do.

I knock on Mrs. Batson's door and she answers it.

"Martin," she says. "Billy's not here. He's gone to the show with some boys from choir."

"Mrs. Batson," I say. "There's a bad man at choir and he's going to try and hurt Billy."

Mrs. Batson lets me in the house. I've never been in here before.

I tell some about Mr. George and me. Not all. Not much. I'm too ashamed. Just enough. I tell her Billy's in the show with Mr. George. She grabs her purse.

"Let's go," she says. And we hurry out the door and down the street.

We're the only ones not celebrating.

Laughing and crying, kissing and hugging, shouting and climbing, cannons and air raid sirens, loud radios and record players turned up full, throwing everything up in the air, riding on the roofs of cars and streetcars, drums and baseball bats and tin pans, homemade costumes, men on crutches, kids in bathing suits in the rain, butter pails to pound, "Hail, hail, the gang's all here!" An old woman is crying against a post. Smoke bombs, toilet paper streamers, firemen, police, and the crowds sing "Roll out the barrel, we'll have a barrel of fun!"

Mrs. Batson buys two tickets and we go into the Français theater. On the screen Abbott and Costello are marching with all the soldiers. When all the soldiers turn left Costello turns right by mistake. Everybody in the theater is laughing.

"Billy! Billy!" Mrs. Batson calls out. "Billy, where are you?"

People in the seats are telling her to sit down. Sit down and shut up. We go right up to the back. I see Mr. George get up and go out the aisle on the far side and run down the stairs. Billy is sitting there. We go in to him. He's crying.

We say come with us we're going home.

Mr. George has disappeared. Run away.

Back at the Batsons' house I tell Mrs. Batson and Billy more about Mr. George and Heney Park.

I feel like we're in a movie. Billy is Captain Marvel and I'm Alan Ladd. When I'm explaining to Mrs. Batson, she's Veronica Lake or maybe Dorothy Lamour or maybe Barbara Stanwyck or maybe Judy Garland. I tell some more about what happened in Heney Park. I let it out bit by bit as the movie camera goes around us sitting there. I'm not me saying this. I'm Alan Ladd so it's all right. I tell some more. Not all. Not everything. Just some. Now there's dramatic movie music playing in my head. Tell more. Tell all. Enough.

Now Billy tells. About being in the show with Mr. George. It's the same with Billy. What Mr. George did to me. Mrs. Batson is crying. If only Mr. Batson were around. Mr. George did stuff to Billy in the organ pipe loft too.

Now Billy hates Mr. George too.

If only Mr. Batson were around. He could go and maybe kill Mr. George.

Now the movie we're in is changing.

On the wall is a photograph of a handsome man. It's Mr. Batson before he got sick. Mrs. Batson starts telling about him. What he was like. A kind, smart man.

This was before they moved to Papineau Street. Billy was just a baby. Mr. Batson started to get sick. He'd disappear for days. Come home dirty and torn. He got fired from his job at the paper mill and got a job at the slaughterhouse.

The slaughterhouse.

Everything is going slow in Mrs. Batson's and Billy's living room. Everything seems so slow. And getting bigger. The picture on the wall. Mrs. Batson's voice. Before they moved to Papineau. The slaughterhouse. It feels like we're all under water in here.

"And then," Mrs. Batson is saying, her voice getting slower and bigger, "one day he came home, his face bleeding. He'd been in a fight or something, in Strathcona Park, near Baron Strathcona's fountain. His eye was badly damaged. He later lost it. Lost his eye. Had to have a glass eye put in. After that, in the hospital he attacked some people and he was arrested and put away eventually — brain disease...very sad..."

Mrs. Batson's voice trailing away...

My granny!

Oh, Granny it was you wasn't it? You were so brave. You stopped suddenly and turned around near Baron Strathcona's fountain and you...

Should I tell them, Granny, that it was you?

I wish you were alive and here right now to help me! To help us!

23

Crown Imperial

WHILE I'M getting ready for church, putting on my good shirt, my mother's moaning on the bed. She's talking about when Phil was born. When I was born.

"It was the hottest day of the year that day when you twins were born. Everything was sticking to everything. I could see the sweat on the doctor's face. The nurse's uniform was soaking wet. I could hardly breathe it was so hot. In that room at the Grace Hospital there was only one window. No breeze at all. They had a fan blowing but it was just blowing more hot air in. And then the doctor said to put an ice bag on my head but they were out of ice so they were putting cold cloths on me...then they put you twins on me, one in each arm and everything was soaked...

"You and then Phil..."

While she's talking I'm looking in her good drawer where I'm not supposed to look unless she's there.

My father's out in the yard with Phil.

The drawer that smells of perfume where she keeps her best things. Secret silk handkerchiefs and lace and braid and brooches and barrettes and letters and a long hat pin with a carved head. This little drawer about the size of a shoe box in Lefebvre's Shoe Market slides in and out as quiet as satin.

It's the best part of the house, this drawer.

When I was a little kid I wanted to get in and live in this drawer. Crawl inside it and stay there in the dark and never come out. With the perfume and the silk and the letters that smell like Blue Grass perfume.

Away from Phil.

On my way out the door I grab Granny's umbrella.

I knock on Billy's door and we take off for church choir.

We have a plan.

Nobody knows this but Billy and me, but we've quit choir.

We're never going back. We don't care what anybody says.

We don't walk the usual way. We don't want to come to the back of the church where Mr. Skippy or the choir boys or Mr. George will see us. And we don't want to be early.

There's a big crowd going to church this Sunday. Biggest crowd ever. The church is full. It's because of the end of the war.

The sign outside the front of the church says this:

A DAY OF NATIONAL THANKSGIVING

TODAY A SPECIAL PIPE ORGAN RECITAL

CROWN IMPERIAL

BY

SIR WILLIAM WALTON

ORGANIST:

MR. THEODORE DONALD SAMUEL GEORGE

Theodore Donald Samuel? Read everything. What a name! T.D.S. George. A name we hate.

Billy knows all about the piece, CROWN IMPERIAL, that Mr. George is going to play. Mr. George is very proud of his playing. Specially this. On this day of National Thanksgiving. Billy has turned the pages for him when he practiced over and over again. Billy knows all about CROWN IMPERIAL.

Now the people are all in church and we can hear the organ and now the choir singing and carrying the cross in to take their places.

O God our help in ages past

I sing along like Bing Crosby. So does Billy.

Now we hear the Reverend start the service.

Now we go around the back of the church and in and down and then up the side stairs to the organ loft.

I lift Billy up and he reaches the key to the door. We open it and go into the pipe room and close the quiet door. We can see through the slats in the wall Mr. George down there sitting at the organ. We can see Mr. Skippy and the choir. We can see Reverend and quite a bit of the audience.

But nobody can see us because we're in the dark.

Billy told me all about the piece Mr. George is going to play for everybody. The piece he's so proud of. CROWN IMPERIAL.

Look at him sitting there. He can hardly wait to show the hundreds of people out there what a great and wonderful player he is.

CROWN IMPERIAL is about eight or nine minutes long. It was composed to celebrate the crowning of King Edward number eight but he quit just before they could crown him so they played it for his brother King George when they gave him the crown instead.

Maybe Mr. George thinks he's King George, sitting there. He can hardly wait to blow these Sandy Hillers right out of their seats with CROWN IMPERIAL.

Billy told me the piece starts off with the TOCCATA, a big wild loud exciting show-offy part for about two and a half minutes and then it goes quieter and nobler and majestic into the PROCESSIONAL where the king probably walks up to get his crown but then Mr. George gets to play the TOCCATA again only even bigger this time and then the PROCESSIONAL over again this time more noble and majestic and then the CODA gets played. The big finish, Billy calls it. In the CODA you think it's going to end but it never does.

And there's one long high note that sounds like a trumpet that is played so that you think that the CODA is actually over but it's not.

"It's never over until it's over," Mr. George told Billy.

That's when he had Billy up here in the organ loft and showed him the exact pipe for that one long high note.

Poor Billy…

What Mr. George made him do up here.

Mr. George loves this part best of all. The big finish. He loves it when the audience thinks it's over but it's not. It's Mr. George, the boss of the whole audience. Mr. George will tell them when it's over. He's the boss. He's the king. Mr. King George.

Six times he plays that long, long trumpet note which is a very high C, says Billy. Five times. Each time you think it's over but it's not. Then, finally, the sixth time, it is actually over.

Billy takes me to the pipe that is one of the smaller ones. There's a piece of tape stuck on the side of the pipe. You can barely see it in the almost dark room.

The most important pipe. "Trumpet-C" the tape says.

This is Mr. George's main note.

We whisper, Billy and me, into each other's ears, going over our plan. Everything's ready.

I'm holding my granny's umbrella. I show Billy the sharp end.

"I have to tell you something, Billy," I whisper into Billy's ear.

"What?" whispers Billy into my ear.

"Remember your mother said your father was in a fight or something and got his eye poked out?" I whisper.

"Yes?" whispers Billy in my ear.

"It was my granny who did it. He tried to attack her and she poked this sharp end of this umbrella in his eye."

"Your granny?"

"Yes."

Billy stares at the long sharp point. He feels it with his fingers. Touches on it. There are tears on Billy's cheeks.

"I'm sorry," I whisper. "I'm sorry it was her who hurt your daddy."

"It's okay, Martin," whispers Billy. "It's not your fault."

"Was he really once a nice man?" I whisper in Billy's ear.

"That's what my mother told me," Billy whispers. "But I don't remember."

"Maybe he wanted to be but he couldn't," I say, forgetting to whisper.

"Maybe," whispers Billy. "Or maybe not."

"Are you sad, Billy?" I whisper.

"No!" says Billy. "SHAZAM!" says Billy. "Let's get Mr. George!" says Billy, forgetting to whisper.

Reverend is starting his sermon now.

We go over our plan again.

It will happen during the CODA, the last part. The CODA is one minute and twenty seconds long. Not a long time to get the job done.

I'm looking out at all the people. I don't know anybody

in this audience. There's nobody here from Lowertown. These people are all from Sandy Hill. They're all wearing pretty nice clothes. The Sandy Hillers. And they're all looking at Reverend doing his sermon. They're looking at him but they don't seem to be listening to him.

Some of them look like they're going to fall over. Go to sleep. Reverend has a very boring voice. They always have a nice sleep when he does his sermon.

Now Reverend says he's going to deliver a short sermon today because he wants to leave room for the very special presentation on this day of National Thanksgiving — Mr. T.D.S. George on our wonderful pipe organ playing CROWN IMPERIAL by Sir William Walton, Master of the King's Music.

Now I think I see the ketchup lady and the turkey lady.

There's one more hymn and a few more prayers and the service is just about over. The choir doesn't sound very good, I don't think, without me and Billy in it.

Mr. George is going to start playing. He raises his arms up in the air and attacks the organ keys like he's an animal attacking its prey. Now he's playing the TOCCATA like mad, waving his head around and raising his shoulders and throwing his chest in and out! The sound here in the pipe room makes you feel like your teeth are going to fall out.

"Look at him," Billy yells in my ear. "He didn't act like that when he was practicing."

Darce the Arse is turning the pages for Mr. George. Darce the Arse will be Mr. George's next victim in Imbro's Restaurant and then Heney Park.

The audience is wide awake now.

Who could sleep through this?

They're all watching Mr. George writhing and squirming and stretching while he's playing. Some of them are pointing. They think he's strange.

Now the grace and majesty of the PROCESSIONAL gets Mr. George moving around on his organ bench like he's some kind of a dancer or somebody trying to kiss the air...

Now the TOCCATA again, bigger now, noisier and then the PROCESSIONAL again and now...

"Get ready," says Billy.

The audience looks like they're wondering what's going to happen now. Mr. George starts the CODA. He looks like he's going to explode.

He has a hundred eyes. His little jaws are working up and down. The reddish brown hair that grows down both cheeks nearly to his chin looks like fangs. His long arms and fingers are moving up and down and across the keyboards and reaching to push and pull the organ stops and tap the buttons so fast that he seems to have many arms and his legs with the seven wounds are dangling and feeling and probing under the organ on the pedals in so many directions that he seems to have more than two.

He doesn't look human.

Mr. George plays the first high Trumpet-C.

"Now!" says Billy and he taps the Trumpet-C sleeve down two inches.

The second of the six high C notes of the CODA is

now too high. It sounds like somebody just stabbed some-body in the stomach with a rusty butcher knife.

The audience's mouths fall open. They can't believe their ears. Mr. George is looking at his keys. He looks like he's been struck by lightning.

I grab my granny's umbrella and start on the bigger pipes, the middle notes, bring down each sleeve as far as I can.

Now the CODA sounds like a war.

I pull down more sleeves. All these notes are now too high.

Mr. George keeps playing. He looks like he has both hands inside bees' nests. No matter what he does, it sounds horrible. He's trying different chords. He won't quit. Granny's umbrella pulls down more sleeves.

The third high C is a strangling cat screaming.

The CODA is now an earthquake.

People in the audience are covering their ears. Some people are trying to leave. Kids are screaming.

The fourth and fifth high C sound like all the sickness in the world and the CODA is now an atomic bomb.

Mr. George is frothing around his mouth.

He's still playing, trying different keys, different but-tons. I'm pulling down every sleeve I can with my granny's umbrella handle. Fifteen, sixteen, seventeen.

The last high C is a volcano. The walls of the church are rumbling. The stained-glass windows are shaking. The people are pushing and stumbling to get out of their rows. The world is coming to an end.

Mr. George is finished. The last awful chord rings off the walls and ceiling like a dying monster.

Mr. George sits there. He looks like he's been shot.

The Sandy Hillers are yelling, "Oh my God!" and stumbling out the door. Reverend is trying to calm people down.

Billy and me, we're hypnotized now by what we've done.

Now Mr. George suddenly stands up.

He looks right up at the organ loft. He's looking right at us but he can't see us through the slats. He moves.

"Let's go!" I say to Billy. "He's coming!"

"SHAZAM!" says Billy.

We head out and into the hall. Too late! He's coming up the stairs two at a time. The only place to hide is behind the open door.

He's breathing very hard. Now he stops breathing. He's right beside us on the other side of the door. He goes quiet into the pipe room.

"I know you're there, Batson. And maybe O'Boy too, eh? My two summer boys. Well, what you did to Mr. George's piece that he worked so hard on wasn't very nice! Was it? I know you're in there hiding. Why don't you come out and confess to Mr. George? Come on now. The fun is over. Let's have a little talk…"

I have the key to the door in the left pocket of my shorts. When Mr. George is far enough in the room, Billy and me, we slam the door shut and I lock it with the key.

Then we run.

Outside the church the Sandy Hillers are in shock.

"That organist must be crazy!"

"If my ears are ruined I'm going to sue him."

"Where did Skippy Skidmore get a useless tool like that!"

"They say that he likes to fiddle with little boys!"

"Reverend should fire the likes of him!"

All of a sudden I say to Billy, "I forgot my granny's umbrella!"

"You can't go back!" says Billy.

"I have to," I say. "I can't lose that umbrella!"

I run down the back stairs past the choir boys coming up.

"Boy O'Boy," they're saying as I push past them on the stairs. "Where ya been, O'Boy?" "You're late O'Boy!" "You shoulda heard Mr. George's special recital!" "It sounded like when an insane asylum burns down!"

I go up the side stairs. Granny's umbrella is on the floor outside the locked door. I go and pick it up.

"I can see you, O'Boy!" whispers Mr. George. "It was you!" I can see one of his awful multiple eyes at the keyhole.

"No!" I say. I feel like shoving the pointy sharp end of the umbrella into the keyhole.

"I'm going to catch you, O'Boy. And when I do, I'm going to hurt you! I'm going to hurt you in a way you'll never forget. I'll find you. I'll find you and I'll get you. And when I do, you're going to be a very, very sorry boy!

A beautiful boy. But you won't be beautiful anymore! I'll take away that beauty from you!"

You already have, Mr. George.

I leave with my granny's umbrella.

Mr. George is pounding on the door.

"Don't sleep at night, O'Boy! I'll be thinking of you, my beautiful Boy O'Boy!" he screams.

24

Bounty

THE TROOP ship, the *Andrea Doria*, came home to Montreal yesterday. Buz will be here this afternoon! At the Union Station! He'll get off the train at one o'clock!

Buz! The wounded war hero! Our Buz!

I can tell him about Mr. George. I think I will tell him.

I'm minding Phil out in the yard. I'm practicing on him. Pretending he's Buz.

"Buz," I say to Phil, "there's a man at choir, the organist for the summer. He was always being nice to me, giving me money and buying me ice cream sundaes at Imbro's."

Phil's nose is running. He's trying to stick a stick that he has in my eye.

Start again.

"Buz, a man at choir cut a piece of his cape so the choir cat wouldn't have to move."

Phil is trying to stab my cat Cheap with the stick. Cheap runs under the back shed.

"Buz, the organist at choir said he'd give me one of his war medals if… Buz, would you give away one of your war medals to some kid?"

Better go in. My father's home for lunch and there's arguing. Sometimes if I'm there they'll stop for a while.

My mother has burned a pot of macaroni and cheese on the stove. The kitchen is full of smoke. Phil is howling and choking. My father takes him out in the yard and puts him on his long rope. My mother is at the kitchen table. She's leaning back. Her belly is a way out.

"Any time now," she says. "Please, God! Or why don't we wait until it gets just a little bit hotter!"

I slip out the front and call on Billy and we head over Angel Square and up to the Byward Market and up to the Union Station. At the station there's Laflammes running around and Lenny Lipshitz and a bunch of people from Cobourg Street all probably there to welcome home Buz.

There's a band getting ready to play on the steps in the station going down to where the trains are. There's a huge crowd of people carrying flowers and babies and flags.

Now everybody's yelling,"The train is here! The train has arrived! The troops are home!"

Now the station man pulls open the big iron gates and we see some soldiers and sailors walking in from the platform carrying big duffel bags on their shoulders. People start walking toward them. They start walking faster. Now people are running into each other's arms. There's squealing and crying and laughing. Now more sailors and some airmen but no Buz yet.

Behind us, on the stairs, the band starts playing.

But there's something else exciting happening. People are stumbling down the stairs, sliding down the brass railings.

Everybody's yelling about money. Somebody giving money away. Somebody crazy. A crazy old guy throwing money around. A nutty millionaire is giving away fifty-dollar bills! Anybody in uniform! Hurry, he's down over there! It's crazy McLean from Merrickville! The millionaire nut from Merrickville is in town and he's gone berserk! He's giving everybody in uniform a fifty-dollar bill! My stars! Hurry!

The crowd is moving this way and that way all of a sudden, like minnows all together.

The soldiers and sailors and airmen coming through the gate are laughing and cheering. Somebody's giving them fifty dollars. Come see! Come see!

Then I see Buz. Then I see Mrs. Sawyer running and hugging Buz. Now the nut millionaire is going over to Buz. Right up to him. Gives him a fifty-dollar bill. Buz salutes him and smiles his handsome smile. Buz has a cast on his wrist. His war wound.

I run up to Buz. So does Billy. Buz shakes hands with us. He's bigger, a lot bigger than when he left. Now he gives us big hugs. He's with two other guys. Two friends of his — big sailors. He tells us their names. They hug Mrs. Sawyer. They have nobody to hug. They have to take another train up to Maniwaki. Somebody will hug them up there.

I can hardly pay attention to all of it. I'm just looking at Buz.

Oh, Buz! We thought you'd never...does your wrist hurt...did your plane crash...were you scared, Buz...were you...did you get your medals, Buz...

Now Buz is looking over my shoulder. He turns me around. He puts his air force cap on me. He straightens it. It's too big. Like my shoes.

Here comes the millionaire again, right for us!

He's got a fistful of fifties!

"Salute!" Buz says. "Salute him!"

I salute. The millionaire gives me a fifty-dollar bill out of his fist. He steps back and looks me up and down.

"And here's another fifty for the shoes! That's quite the uniform there, son!" he says. And moves on.

A hundred dollars! My horrorscope! My bounty!

I give back Buz's cap and stuff the money in the left pocket of my shorts.

We start to walk a few steps toward the band on the stairs. The cymbals are crashing and the drums pounding and the trombones are flashing in the bright sunlight pouring in the high windows of the Union Station.

Now there's something else flashing that sinks my heart and makes my knees weak and my stomach roll over. I swallow hard.

It's a pair of glasses flashing in the sunbeams from the high windows of the Union Station.

It's Mr. George. He's looking at me and Billy.

25

Sorriest Organ Player

MY MOTHER'S sitting on the bed. She's wiping her hands and face with a cold cloth I just got her. Now she wants her Blue Grass Eau de Parfum and I get it for her out of the smooth-as-satin drawer. She squirts a squirt of Blue Grass on each wrist. I take the bottle and before I put it back in the drawer I squirt it at Phil. Phil roars.

"Don't do that," my mother says. "You know he hates that!"

Too bad.

What are we going to do with Phil once the baby comes to live in Lowertown?

"Go and ask Billy if he'll mind Phil for a few minutes while you go and get your father. Because I think it's just about time for me to go to the hospital. And I can't chase after Phil right now."

"Billy hates Phil! He's afraid of him!" I say.

"Tell him it's just for half an hour. Tell him I'll give him a dime."

"Never mind the dime," I say. "I'll give him a *dollar*! I'm rich, remember?"

"I want you to hide that money. When I get back from the hospital with the baby I'll put it in the bank for you. And don't tell your father about it. He'll probably hear about it anyway but let's keep it a secret as long as we can…"

I give the two fifty-dollar bills to Mrs. Batson to keep for me and Billy goes to mind Phil and I flap slap up to the Lafayette beer parlor to get my father.

Yesterday at the station Mr. George started walking toward Billy and me. Could he see that we were with Buz and the two sailors and Mrs. Sawyer and some Laflammes? Maybe not. It was so crowded that he wasn't sure. That's why he was coming so slow.

"Buz!" I said. Buz was talking to Mrs. Sawyer and some people.

"Buz!" I said. Buz didn't hear me.

"Buz!" I said, reaching up to his ear and pulling on the hard cast on his wrist.

"Buz," I said. He was listening now.

"See that man, the man with the thick glasses and the reddish brown hair coming over to us? That man is the choir organist and he put his hand in my pants and he made me do dirty things in Heney Park one night with him and he did Billy too."

Buz heard every word I said.

Mr. George saw now that Billy and me were with some people. He was coming over almost sideways, being real polite.

"Excuse me, flight lieutenant," he says to Buz. "I'd like to have, if I may, a few words with these two fine lads from our choir about their recent attendance. It won't take long, just a little chat. Can you come along, boys?"

Buz says something to the two big sailors and steps up. He puts out his cast hand as if to shake hands with Mr. George and when Mr. George looks down at the cast Buz's other hand shoots out and plucks Mr. George's glasses off his face.

Mr. George now can hardly see.

"Hold him there," Buz says to the two sailors, and they grab Mr. George's arms and pull them back. Nobody seems to notice, it's so crowded. Mrs. Sawyer is chatting with some people and the whole place is still buzzing about the nut millionaire and the band is blaring away.

Buz holds the glasses up near Mr. George's ear.

"Listen to this," he says and snaps the glasses in two. "That's what's going to happen to the rest of you if you ever bother these boys again."

"My glasses. You broke my glasses…" says Mr. George.

Buz is feeling in Mr. George's jacket and his pants pockets and comes out with his wallet and goes through the wallet. He takes out a card.

Buz reads off the card.

"T.D.S. George, 428 Rideau Street, Apartment 1201. Now get this," says Buz. "You never, never go near these boys again. You never have anything to do with them. You don't follow them, you don't talk to them, you don't look at them, you don't even think about them. And if I ever hear about you ever again, I've got your address here and we'll come for you, my friends and I, and you'll wind up the sorriest organ player that ever had a fondness for fiddling with choir boys..."

Buz gave him back his wallet but kept the glasses and the I.D card.

"Away you go now," said Buz.

And away went Mr. George into the crowd...

I go into the tavern and up to my father's table.

"Mother says you better come home. Baby's on the way!" I say, out of breath.

"I'll just finish this beer and I'll be right there," says my father. "I hear you're rich!"

I turn and head toward the door through the smoke and beer fumes and crashing bottles and glasses.

"And tell her not to be in such a rush!" shouts my father to me and gets a big laugh all around the table.

Really funny.

Going home, I'm thinking about when I told Buz all about how Mr. George was wounded in the legs in the war. Buz said it was probably a lie because with that poor eyesight, with those eyes, they would never let him in the army. All lies about being wounded and the woman with the truffles and shooting the German soldier who was squatting under the tree and everything...

"But what about his uniform? He had on an army uniform. And the medals. He had medals," I said to Buz.

"Probably bought them," said Buz.

FOR SALE:
Army uniforms. War Medals.
(ask inside)

Read everything.

Going home, I'm wondering about the baby that's coming. He? She? Two of them? Not another Phil, I hope.

With some of my hundred dollars I'm going to get a really good pair of shoes. The best pair. And they're going to fit! And I'm going to get a new sweater. Not a sweater with the sleeves unraveling. And new pants. Pants with two pockets, left *and* right.

Dramatis Personae

Granny — a beautiful lady who will be with Martin
   forever
Martin O'Boy — a victim
Father — he doesn't care
Mother — tries to care, but can't
Dr. O'Malley — a nodding doctor
Father Fortier — he says the words
Phil — not a normal twin
Cheap — a boy's best friend with one ear
a man — he attacks from the slaughterhouse
Baron Strathcona — just an old baron with a fountain
   named after him
Miss Gilhooly — a teacher who tries to waste time
Grampa — a retired soccer player whose heart is some-
   where else
Mrs. Sawyer — she waits for her son, Buz
Turkey lady — she has blue hair
Ketchup lady — her face is painted
Mrs. Laflamme — mother of Horseball and many others
Mr. Laflamme — the coughing father of all the
   Laflammes
Buz Sawyer — a war hero
Billy Batson — more prey for a predator

Mrs. Batson — a woman of mystery
Lenny Lipshitz — a gambler with a lying face
Lenny Lipshitz's father — rag man
Mr. Lipshitz's horse — he's tired, except during celebrations
Aztecs — they killed the beautiful boy
baby in the belly — it wants to come out and live in Lowertown, or does it?
Mr. Skippy — he likes his summer boys
Billy Batson — the other one in the comics who turns into Captain Marvel by saying SHAZAM!
Captain Marvel — he wears a tight red suit with yellow trim
Dr. Radmore — an animal sadist
Ketchy Balls — another sadist, this time a teacher
Killer Bodnoff — accurate with an ice-ball
Bing Crosby — could cause trouble for a choir boy
Bob Hope — supposed to be funny but isn't
Dorothy Lamour — her nightgown makes Billy say
SHAZAM!
Mr. T.D.S. George — a predator
Billy's father — supposed to be a very nice, kind man
Veronica Lake — she charms men's hearts with her hair-do
Christian Brothers — they wear long black dresses
Abbott and Costello — two funny guys in the movies
drunk shoe salesman — an air-conditioning expert
Lefebvres shoe lady — she gives discounts
Old Faithful — a kicked pail with special contents
St. Alban — martyr

Sheena the jungle girl — not many clothes on

ice house man — a man with a specially shaped head

Dick Dork, Darce the Arse and Dumb Doug — three
foolish summer boys

Fred MacMurray — he looks just like Captain Marvel
except for the clothes

Barbara Stanwyck and Edward G. Robinson — an unhap-
pily married couple

Alan Ladd — Veronica Lake wants to kiss him

Geranium Mayburger and Mr. Blue Cheeks — characters
from Angel Square

Sixpouce and Goliath — different-sized lacrosse players

Yvon Robert and The Mask — two friendly wrestlers who
try to kill each other

Percy Kelso — don't call him Tomato unless you want to
die

Imbro's waitress — she wears a huge pencil in her hair

Old Man Petigorsky — a shoemaker who thinks he's
funny

hundred-year-old fly swatter — "They never knew what
hit 'em!"

Andrews Sisters — they sing to Abbott and Costello

Reverend — he puts the Sandy Hillers to sleep

Sandy Hillers — they get blown out of their church pews

Merrickville Millionaire — he loves a uniform

two big sailors — nobody to hug them just yet